Kildare Library & Arts Service
Seirbhís Leabharlanna & Ealaíone Chill Dara

In the interest of all library members, please
return this item on or before the latest
date shown below. You can renew items
unless they have been requested by another
member. Fines on overdue items will be
charged, including the cost of postage.

Alethea Kontis

The Trix Adventures Book Two
Books of Arilland Volume 6

Cover Design by Rachel Marks
Interior Design by Polgarus Studio

Books of Arilland

Other Titles by Alethea Kontis

Want to know when Alethea has a new book out? Sign up for the newsletter! You'll get brief monthly emails about new releases, book sales, Princess Alethea merchandise, and videos featuring the author princess herself!

Sign up today: http://www.aletheakontis.com

For the children too smart for their own britches
And for the adults who remember being them.

1

The Emissary

 izinia, watch this!" Trix leapt off the branch and flew above the forest floor.

The sparrows would not have called it flying. Squirrels, on the other hand, knew exactly what he meant. Trix stretched out a hand and caught the vine he'd been aiming for. He wrapped his elbow around it and prayed it was sturdy enough to catch his weight.

It was.

With a holler, Trix let the vine carry him into a high arc. He turned a quick somersault in the air, but instead of straightening out for a clean dive, he kept his body pulled into as tight a ball as he could manage. Lizinia's shrieks of joy as he hit the water made him smile.

Once below the dappled surface he stretched out in the water, kicking toward shore. A school of minnows scurried through his hair and a medium-sized trout brushed silkily against his belly. This inlet was warm compared to the cool of the night. The last time he'd been swimming he hadn't needed to breathe air. But that had been a wish, granted and run its course.

Lizinia jumped up and down as he resurfaced. Her gleeful clapping clanked like an enthusiastic cowbell as her gilded palms met again and again.

"Thank you, thank you," he said with great condescension. "That is, without doubt, the largest splash I have ever made in my life." Thanks to Papa Gatto's enchantment, he now possessed the taller, heavier body of a young human man and not the lithe scrawniness of a fey boy the same age.

"My turn!" cried the golden girl.

"You don't think the water will——?" But it was too late. Lizinia had already leapt from her spot on the bank, clothes and all. There was little grace to her entrance, but her splash was epic. Trix gave a proud shriek of his own, blinking salty droplets out of his eyes as his body bobbed up and down in her wake.

He commended himself on discovering this choice spot. He'd just been thinking that they needed a respite after their long day of walking eastward, away from Rose Abbey, along the Impossible Ocean's edge to the legendary home of the King of Eagles. As if he'd been granted another wish, that respite had appeared. Thanks to the magical seawater his angry sister had conjured, what had once been a sheer cliff face now made a magnificently deep swimming hole.

A hole from which Lizinia had still not risen.

A hole into which that girl, entirely covered in gold, had just jumped.

Most people with common sense would have remembered that gold did not float. Trix Woodcutter rarely qualified as "most people."

"Trixie, you are a prize idiot," he said to himself, because neither Peter nor Saturday were there to say it for him. He took a deep breath and dove hard.

The trout, sensing his distress, joined him. The fish swam at his sides, so that he did not have to worry about injuring any of them with his furious kicking. The further they descended, the darker the water became. Trix was wondering how he might find his companion without sight when a bright light burst out from the crescent-shaped bone that hung from a thong around his neck: Wisdom's tooth. A tiny glint reflected back from the shadows. Trix kicked faster in that direction.

Where some might have panicked at such a predicament, Lizinia had simply begun climbing the cliff face. This was one of the things Trix loved most about Lizinia: she was just as happy an adventurer as he.

With a wave of Trix's hand, the trout swam up beneath Lizinia and nestled under her arms, propelling upward with their strong tails. They made faster progress than Lizinia had been making on her own, but their scales continued to slip off Lizinia's slick golden skin. Trix's heart pounded in his chest, desperate for air. He grabbed her hands and tried to pull her up on his own, but even with his new and improved body, Lizinia's gold was easily half again his weight.

Trix caught Lizinia's eye. He forced himself not to be frightened. Just as he was about to lose all hope—and any chance of breathing again—they began to ascend. Trix swam down to Lizinia's feet. Her golden slippers rested upon the backs of two very fine snapping turtles. Her head broke the surface soon after that, and they both gasped for air. After a few deep, blissful breaths, Trix helped pull his companion to the shore.

"Perhaps our next attempt at swimming should be in a shallower pond," she said when she caught her breath.

"Perhaps indeed. Thank you, friends!" Trix patted the heads of the turtles and bid them farewell before turning back to Lizinia. "I'm sorry. I did not think about the gold."

"I didn't think about it either," said Lizinia. "Which is more my fault, since it is my gold."

"I should have at least had the trout check the depth for us."

Lizinia waved her hands and then let them fall to the grass. "Next time."

Trix rolled onto his back, his breath finally slowing to an even rhythm, and thought about how grateful he was that there would *be* a next time. He stared up into the sky and thanked every star scattered there. This had once been one of his favorite pastimes, before the Impossible Ocean and the start of his adventures.

"Were you scared?" he asked.

There was a pause before Lizinia answered. "I think I forgot to be scared. I was too busy trying to climb back up."

Trix smiled. It was the sort of thing *he* would have said. "You just jumped right in and I didn't even think…does that mean you can't take any of your clothes off? Not even your shoes?" When Lizinia had told him the story of how the cats had dipped her in gold, she had said that her greedy mother and sister could not remove her golden clothes, try as they might. But she hadn't mentioned that they couldn't be removed *at all*.

"No," she said. "I don't mind, too much. This is a fine dress, and it protects me from everything."

Trix had enough sisters to know that the tone of her voice hid something. "But?"

From beside him on the grass, he heard Lizinia exhale. "It will sound silly, I know, but I miss colors."

"You could wear a dress over your dress. Or an apron or something."

"That sounds even sillier."

She was right. Outfitting Lizinia would be an unnecessary burden.

"I miss baths, too," she said. "I had high hopes for our swimming adventure."

"As did I," said Trix, though for different reasons. He'd wanted to feel like he was home, just for a little while. He missed the Wood, his family, and the life he'd lived as the boy he wasn't anymore. He sent up a few wistful pleas to the stars. And when his thoughts stopped being selfish and shifted back to Lizinia, he realized he had missed something fairly important.

"Wait. You can't take off your undergarments?"

"Nope." He could tell she was smiling when she said it. How long had she been waiting for him to ask?

"Then how do you…?"

"…void my bowels?"

"I was going to say 'poop,' but yes."

"I just don't," she said. "I didn't realize it for a while after the cats gave me my 'gift,' but eventually it came to me. I don't really need to eat or drink much. Sometimes I go days without it. You may have noticed."

Since his growth spurt, Trix had been eating like a horse. He thought Lizinia's lack of appetite was simply a courtesy. "But you do eat. I've seen you. What happens to it all? Where does it go?"

"I'm...not sure."

"You're not sure?" Trix didn't mean to be purposefully daft, but it did seem the important sort of thing a body should just *know*.

"I think maybe it turns to energy," she said calmly. Mama and most of his sisters would never have humored him this long in such a conversation—another point in Lizinia's favor. "I do know that whatever I eat affects the gold of my skin. The quality—even the color—changes depending on what I consume. I lived off magic apples mostly, back when I lived with the cats, but Papa Gatto would sometimes bring me things on his visits. Nuts make my skin harder. Strawberries give it a reddish tint, if I eat enough of them. Cantaloupes are just horrible."

"What happens to your skin when you eat cantaloupes?"

Lizinia shrugged. "Nothing. They're just horrible."

"Wow."

"What? Trix, you're staring at me."

"And here I thought the stars were amazing."

"It's not amazing. It's just how I am."

"Trust me," said Trix. "To the rest of the world, you're pretty amazing."

"Speaking of amazing..." Lizinia's golden finger pointed into the sky. "What's that?"

Trix turned and propped his head up on one hand. A glow lit the distant horizon to the north, outlining the White Mountains with a feathered aura of green and pink and gold. "I don't know," he said. "But it's beautiful."

They watched the shifting, glittering lights in silence for a while. And then a great roar filled the air. It sounded very far away, which meant it had to have been a *particularly* great roar.

"Was that a bear?" asked Lizinia.

Trix sat up. He grabbed his shirt and pulled it over his head. "No." Trix put his shoes on and then helped the golden girl to her feet. "I've heard that sound. Before I met you. It is the sound of the earth breaking."

"Should we run?"

Trix held fast to Lizinia's hand, but he did not move. The noise had happened, but he felt no vibrations beneath his feet. Not so much as a breath of wind stirred the leaves in the trees of the forest around them. He closed his eyes and searched inside himself for the Fear that Needa the spider had taught him about. There was a sort of...tingle...at the back of his neck and in his belly. This might have been the animal magic inside him telling him *flee*, but his instincts were still not strong enough to know *where*.

A second great roar sounded, loud and long and...angry.

"*That* was not earth," Lizinia said confidently. "That was an animal."

Trix had only ever met one animal legendary enough to make that sound, and the lingworm had been adamant that dragons no longer existed.

"Wait," he cautioned.

Trix should be able to sense *something*. He should be able to feel what nature was telling him. Despite his appearance, only a small piece of Trix was human. The rest him was mostly fey…and mostly Prince of Eagles. But as he'd known nothing about that last bit until a few days ago, that half of him remained useless.

"Um…Trix?" Lizinia's hand squeezed his gently.

"Shh! I'm trying to concentrate."

"Yes, I know that, but…" She sighed. "We have a visitor."

Trix looked at her, and then followed her gaze up into the trees. There on a low branch, lazily waving his tail, was the smoky outline of Lizinia's dearly departed godfather, Papa Gatto.

Trix sneered.

Papa Gatto grinned.

Shivers ran down Trix's spine. A grin on a cat was a disturbingly unnatural thing. Then again, a spectral feline who had the ability to cast spells beyond the grave wasn't particularly natural either.

The cat's fur waved in a wind that wasn't there. One eye disappeared, and then the other, but that grin remained as constant as the crescent moon in a cloud-filled sky. The cat had interviewed Trix at length to decide his fitness for traveling with Lizinia before their initial journey to Rose Abbey. He had not spoken a word to Trix since—though he'd reportedly shared many conversations with Lizinia.

The cat tilted his head, much like Lizinia often did, and then turned and looked deeper into the woods, away from the makeshift shoreline.

"We should go that way," said Lizinia.

In all likelihood, Papa Gatto was right. But the mere presence of the cat aggravated Trix so much that he was hesitant to obey any advice, no matter how wise. Oh, yes, Trix might have been a young man on the outside, but he was definitely still the stubborn, foolish, petulant boy he'd always been on the inside. He opened his mouth, illogical protest already on his tongue, when he felt the earth shift through the soles of his borrowed boots.

Here were the vibrations.

Here was the rumble he knew.

Like it or not, the dormant part of his animal self was going to have to rely on Papa Gatto's spectral guidance. As if he could read Trix's thoughts, the cat's devilish grin grew wider.

"Run," said the cat.

Trix and Lizinia ran. The forest around them began to shift wildly. It wasn't breaking, like it had before—this was more of a *pulling*. Tree trunks stretched, split, and stretched again. Runners of grass sped past their feet like currents in a swollen river. The colors of the autumn leaves began to blur together, reds, golds, and greens shimmering like the lights in the sky.

Trix looked to the sky. It was still black and full of stars, like every other clear night he'd ever witnessed…save for the lightning now shooting colors around them in every direction, as if someone had angered the rainbows and they'd gone to war.

He turned back to the cliff face, curious how soon the water would swallow him this time. Instead, he saw the waves receding. The Impossible Ocean was leaving Arilland as quickly and dramatically as it had come.

Trix slowed his pace. Compared to what he'd been put through during the ocean's arrival, this situation seemed far less dire.

"Trix, what are you doing?" Lizinia cried as he let go of her hand.

"There!" He pointed, and they altered their direction to the great tree he had indicated.

The tree was a massive live oak with multiple trunks. Some spread out like branches low to the ground and some shot into the sky—Trix and Lizinia used the former to climb to the latter. Unlike the other trees in the surrounding forest, this tree would have held its own among the trees of the Wood. Most importantly, this tree was not one of the ones splitting into rainbow blurs around them. It sat tall, steady and strong, like an old grandfather who had no time to be bothered with new magic.

They helped each other high enough to avoid being caught in the surge of land, but not so high that the branches weren't sturdy enough to hold their weight. Trix climbed out further on the limb while Lizinia sat at the base of the branch. She leaned against the trunk and gazed down into the chaos below. The wind tossed her hair wildly about; Trix made sure to stay clear of being whipped by the dangerous strands of gold.

"It's beautiful," she said. "I mean, it's frightening, but it's *beautiful*."

Trix took a moment to appreciate the view. Even if there had existed a similarly safe vantage point when the oceans had come flooding in, the sight would not have been this lovely. Between the water pouring down from the sky and creeping up from the ground there had only been one color: muddy gray. Now, the swirling colors entranced him. Their movement was more of a rush than a roar. Scents of loam and leaves drifted up to them. It was almost...relaxing. The ceaseless rustle tempted him into sleep.

What?

This wasn't time for sleeping, this was time to be awake and exhilarated! But there was no resisting the downward pull of eyelids that suddenly felt like anvils. He opened his mouth to call out to Lizinia, but she could not hear him over the din. It was all he could do to situate himself on the tree limb before he finally lost consciousness.

"Have a care, Trix Woodcutter. It would not do to to have you falling to your death right when I need you most."

Power. The woman's voice that filled his ears was powerful. It reminded him of someone—a member of his family?—but he could not place it.

"I did not intend for us to meet like this, but time is short. Forgive me."

Asking forgiveness instead of getting permission was something Trix himself had done too many times to count. He managed to force his eyes open. His head ached as he strained to focus in the new light.

"Where am I?"

This was no place he had seen before. No longer up a tree in the dark, color-melting forest, he now found himself stretched out on a grassy knoll. Wildflowers and clover sprouted in clumps throughout the meadow and brought with them the scent of spring...not autumn, as it should have been. Fat clouds floated by in a sky that seemed to have no sun—the world here was lit with a strange, unearthly blue light.

Trix dug his fingernails into the ground. It all felt so *real*, even though he knew it couldn't be. And then he realized what was happening. "No, no, no, no, *no*. ABSOLUTEY NO MORE VISIONS!"

The woman shrugged. "Too late."

Trix's previous experience with visions had revealed his birthmother to him. She'd visited him multiple times, compelling him to poison his family and run away from home, all while she'd lain ensorcelled by a sleeping spell. He hadn't seen her since visiting her body at Rose Abbey.

"This is ridiculous," Trix said angrily. "A person should at least have control over his own mind."

"I agree," the woman answered. "One day, you and I will have a chat with the gods about such things. But this is not that day. Something terrible has happened."

Trix considered all that he'd been through since running away from the towerhouse, culminating with his being trapped by a vision in a tree surrounded by furious magic. "Something terrible is always happening."

He half expected the powerful woman to scold him for the flippant remark, as Mama would have, but instead she gave him the finest of smiles. She possessed incredible beauty—his eldest sister being the most beautiful woman in the world made Trix a more than adequate judge of such things. It was difficult to look away. Her eyes were a shocking violet that seemed to change with the light, flashing with either blue or red. Her brows arched dramatically above them like the sweep of a butterfly's wing, lending her countenance a sense of both the wicked and the wonderful. Both her brows and her hair were black as the night and scattered with stars that seemed to twinkle—as her eyes did—whenever she moved. She wore a dress of flowers and fog and spidersilk and shadow.

The moment Trix put all the pieces together, he was too shocked to reply. What in the world did the Faerie Queen want with him? If this even was the world…on this grassy mound, surrounded by a ring of mushrooms. Even the mushrooms bowed, bonnets to the queen.

"Once upon a time," the Faerie Queen began, much in the same way Papa always did, "there were dragons in this world. But that was a very long time ago."

"So I've heard," said Trix.

"Along with them, high in the White Mountains, lived a race of people. They dedicated themselves to the beasts. In turn, the dragons allowed them the use of their magic."

"I assume these people died off along with the dragons."

"As did we all," said the Faerie Queen. "But a dragon has awoken, and all fey magic beneath the Hill has been bound. I cannot think that these two things are unrelated."

"My Aunt Joy is in Faerie! My sister Wednesday is her apprentice. They are the most powerful fey I know. Why can't you ask them for help?"

"They have been magically bound as well."

Trix squinted at the vision. "If your magic is bound too, how can we be having this conversation?"

"At full strength, I could have transported you straight here with but a thought. This is the last of my power." The Faerie Queen indicated their surroundings.

"Why me?"

"You are the Boy Who Talks to Animals," she said. "And with the fey magic bound, anyone under the Hill with animal magic has been turned into a beast. They cannot talk to us, nor can they talk to each other. Soon there will be nothing but chaos, and such an imbalance can tear this world apart." The Faerie Queen clasped her hands together as she made her plea. "I want to make you my Emissary, Trix Woodcutter. You must speak for the animals. Save Faerie. And save the world."

The longer the Faerie Queen spoke to him, the more dire he began to realize the situation was. Trix was supposed to be searching for his birthfather, but the King of Eagles would need to remain a stranger for a little while longer. The fate of the world hung in the balance! It's not like there was another Boy Who Talked to Animals that could take his place...

"I accept," he said eagerly.

"You must come immediately," said the queen.

The urgent need to spring into action overwhelmed the instinctive tingling he'd felt in the animal parts of himself. They were so far away from Faerie! He had to leave *now*. "I have a companion, but I'm sure she won't mind."

"Gods bless you, child. Now, you will need to arm yourselves."

"Lizinia's covered in gold, so she doesn't need a weapon," he said. "I have a dagger. But I have never needed anything more than my wits in the company of animals."

"Even with your skills, it is not safe here. These are more than animals, my dear. They are fey men gone mad, trapped in bodies they cannot escape."

Unlike some of his sisters, Trix had very little knowledge of weapons. Thursday had given him a bow…but even if he'd had it with him, it would have been too small for his new man-sized body. "I do know some archery," he said, "But I do not have a bow, or the arrows to shoot from it."

The Faerie Queen read his mind before he could make so much as a suggestion. "Anything shot from a mundane bow will not help you here. These beasts are too powerful." The Faerie Queen looked to the sky, as if checking the position of the sun to see how much time had passed, only there was no sun in these strange azure heavens. "Look for an island. You will find a woman who can provide you with what you need."

"Thank you." He hated that this side quest would delay their arrival in Faerie, but he appreciated the queen's straightforwardness. Visions had a tendency to be poetic and cryptic. "But I have to ask—"

"I know you still have many questions, but my magic is fading, so I have brought you someone who might be able to answer them." The Faerie Queen, her dress, and the Hill itself began to sparkle around the edges. "Save us, Trix Woodcutter. Save us all."

"—WHO WOKE THE DRAGON?" Trix called after her, but she was already gone. The sound of his own cry woke him out of his vision-state. He wobbled on the tree branch; Lizinia caught him before he could fall.

Trix blinked once, twice. Shook his head, trying to clear the cobwebs from his magic-addled brain. The rush of the magic had stopped; there was nothing below them now but forest, as far as the eye could see. In his hands was a small, ginger-furred rodent.

It nosed about, sniffed his hands and shirt, and then looked up at Trix with cloudy, blind eyes.

"Yes, yes," said the brownie, "Judging by your smell, your sister. Yes, yes. Your sister woke the dragon."

2

The Brownie that Fell from the Sky

"y sister?" Trix asked the brownie.

"Your sister?" Lizinia asked Trix. "Which sister?"

Monday, Wednesday, Thursday, Saturday, Sunday…even Friday…all of Trix's sisters were capable of doing a thing like waking a dragon, but he knew which would be first on his list.

"Bad-tempered giant in a skirt," said the brownie. His two overly-large, pointed teeth gave him somewhat of a lisp. "Yes, yes. Strong. Growly. Bad-tempered. Ears like mine."

"Saturday," said Trix, his guess confirmed. Mostly. Saturday normally wouldn't be caught dead in a skirt. And what was the bit about ears? Brownies' ears were wide set and came to a point, unlike rats. This brownie had a distinct notch in one of his ears—well-healed over, definitely not a new wound. This brownie must have been quite the scrapper in his tribe. Saturday was a fighter, too.

"What does he say?" asked Lizinia. "What did Saturday do?"

"Woke a dragon, apparently," answered Trix.

"Yes, yes. And broke the world, and killed the witch, yes. Fell off the mountain and fought the dragon. Fell from the sky we did, yes, yes. And then she remade the world again before we landed." The brownie's nose stretched over the edge of Trix's lap. He sniffed and shuddered, his hindquarters trying to hide a tail that wasn't there. There was no way the blind animal could have seen how high up in the tree they were—he must have sensed their location some other way. "Remade. Yes, yes. Whole and hale down here. Not up there, no. Not all rescued. But we few, yes. We few, we flew."

Very little of this made any sense to Trix, and he hadn't the first clue how to translate any of it for Lizinia. But one of the brownie's rambling comments stood out among the rest. "Saturday broke the world? *She's* the one who called the ocean?"

"Don't know about an ocean, no, no," said the brownie. "Time itself does not reach the Top of the World, no, but the shaking did. Time itself could not destroy the Great Mountain, no, but she did. Broken, now. Broken. Yes, yes."

Trix was even more confused. "Time is broken?"

"No, no. The mountain," the brownie clarified, as if Trix were daft. Trix was beginning to feel as if he were.

"From the look on your face, I should be glad I don't understand animal-speak," said Lizinia.

Trix squeezed the bridge of his nose. He ran a hand through his hair and tugged on a few strands, not completely convinced that he wasn't still trapped in the vision. "I'm not entirely sure I understand it either."

"Take your time," she said. "I can wait to hear the story."

"I expect it will be a long one," said Trix.

"Then we should get out of this tree," said the golden girl. "I think it's safe to descend now."

"Good idea. This might go more smoothly on solid ground."

"Yes, yes," said the brownie. "Born at the Top of the World, yes. A lover of heights, no. No, no. Not a lover."

Gingerly, Trix lifted the brownie and placed him inside the traveling pack he'd acquired at Rose Abbey. The pack that had been lovingly and smartly prepared by none other than the legendary (and exceptionally not-dead) Jack Woodcutter himself.

"Make yourself comfortable," he said to the brownie. "We'll be out of this tree shortly."

Lizinia made better time out of the tree than Trix did, as she fell most of the way. Thankfully, her gilded skin protected her like an armor. She got to her feet at the bottom, brushed off her knees where they'd muddied themselves in the landing, and waited for Trix to join her.

"So," she said when his feet hit the ground. "Somewhere in all that noise was a dragon?" She waved to indicate the forest around them. The trees were solid and steady now, and there were many more of them. They were each thick with old growth, and their bark bore no scars from colorful lightning. The only muddled rainbow left was that of the autumn leaves rustling as nonchalantly as if they'd been on branches there all along. The soft breeze carried with it the scent of chill and loam. Apart from the notable absence of wildlife, and seawater, everything about this tranquil woodland setting was magicless and positively…normal.

"It…well…hmm." Trix really wasn't sure where to begin.

"Okay, forget the dragon. What exactly happened to you up there? You went all stiff and wouldn't answer me, and I was worried you'd fall out of the tree. And where did…I'm sorry, I'm not familiar with that breed of animal. It looks a bit like a rat, but no rat I've ever seen. A mole, perhaps?"

"Brownie," said Trix, thankful for the ability to answer at least one of her questions with complete certainty.

"Thank you. Where did the brownie come from?"

Trix looked to the sky. "Let's make camp," he decided. "It's already late, and we have quite a journey ahead of us in the morning."

Lizinia put her hands on her hips. "I get the feeling we are no longer seeking the King of the Eagles."

"That feeling would be correct," said Trix.

"May I ask where we'll be heading?"

"Faerie," he said. "The queen needs our help."

Lizinia tilted her head at him, in that way Lizinia always did, and Trix braced himself.

"I'll search for firewood," she said. "With luck, some of these magical trees will have shed a few magically fire-starting branches in their race to magically appear."

Trix caught her hand before she could walk away. His sisters would have scolded him for evading questions and changing their direction mid-course. Lizinia, he thanked the stars again, was not one of his sisters. "I just told you we're heading to Faerie. Which, if you've ever seen a map at all, you would know is about a million miles in the opposite direction from the way we were headed."

Lizinia sighed. "It was too much to hope that we were just around the corner."

"Wait. You're not mad?"

Lizinia fixed him with those amber irises. "Are you not Trix Woodcutter, Prince of Arilland, Prince of Eagles, and Boy Who Talks to Animals?"

It was an impressive list of titles when she put it all together like that. "I am," he said humbly.

"Then I'm right where I'm supposed to be," she said. "You told me the risks of adventuring with you at Rose Abbey. I accepted that risk with the full knowledge of what I was getting myself into. Your path is my path. What care I where the road leads so long as it's interesting?"

Trix pulled her closer and kissed her cool, golden cheek. "I have not stopped being glad that you chose to accompany me, Goldilocks."

"I hope you never do," she said proudly as she tromped off into the forest.

Trix set his pack gingerly on the ground and opened the flap. A great burp greeted him. It seemed the brownie had found the food and helped himself.

"I eat when I get nervous," said the brownie. "Yes, yes."

Trix would have to take that into account on their journey. He lifted the brownie out of the pack. "Forgive me for not introducing myself before, friend. I'm Trix Woodcutter."

"Yes, yes. The Boy Who Talks to Animals." There was a time

when Trix would have been surprised that his personal prophecy extended all the way to the Top of the World, but that time was long since past. "I am Trebald."

Trix did not know much about the White Mountains and the Top of the World, but he knew enough about brownies to know that they always belonged to a clan. "And which is your clan?"

"Clan, no, no," said Trebald, and then he thought some more. "Wait. Bor Alis. Yes, yes. Bor Alis clan."

"Forgive me," said Trix. "I'm not familiar with that clan."

"They may call us something else down here," said Trebald. "As we were the only clan at the Top of the World, we never used the title. No, no."

Bringing the brownie down to earth seemed to have worked figuratively as well as literally. Calmer now, and sated by the food from Trix's pack, Trebald was far less agitated and much more coherent. He was also a great deal sleepier. Trix would have been sleepy too, if he'd had to journey from the Top of the World.

"So you've met my sister? She's all right?"

The brownie opened his mouth wide in a great yawn. "Yes, yes. And no, no." His cloudy eyes bore into Trix, seeing but not seeing. "Not all right. I'm sorry."

Trix thought about calling to Lizinia, but he was frozen in place. He didn't like being alone when he heard bad news. Any bad news. Especially this sort of bad news. He took in a deep breath and held it as the brownie spoke again.

"I bit her. Yes, yes. Scared, ungrateful Trebald. Bit to blood, I did. Yes, yes. So very sorry."

Trix exhaled. "You...*bit* her."

"Yes, yes."

"How many times?" He tried not to laugh as he spoke; he didn't want the brownie to think Trix's amusement was at his expense.

"Once. Yes, yes, just the once."

Trix pressed his lips together tightly. He'd bitten Saturday himself a time or two in younger days, and she had absolutely deserved it. But she had never been in danger of dying from it. Indeed, Saturday wouldn't have been in danger from far worse a wound—she had a destiny, and until she fulfilled it, Fate had rendered her invincible.

"So she was alive when you left her."

"Yes, yes." The brownie bedded down in a drift of multicolored leaves. "Angry and alive. The human and the horse were alive too, but not angry at all. No, no." The brownie yawned again and his words drifted away as he succumbed to sleep. "I didn't bite them."

Trix patted the fur of his new companion and leaned back against the trunk of the great tree. Lizinia returned before too long, her arms filled with enough sticks for a small fire. Trix pulled the flint from his pack, and they made short work of it—in no time, they were huddled close around the small blaze.

"We're getting good at this," said Lizinia.

"Just gives us more time to get good at other things," Trix said automatically. It was a favorite expression of Mama's.

"Poor thing," Lizinia cooed over Trebald's sleeping body. "Did you ever sort out his story?"

"It sounds like Saturday created the ocean and somehow ended up in the White Mountains at the Top of the World. Then she killed a witch, woke a dragon, and destroyed the mountain. In that order."

"My goodness. How did they escape?"

"I'm a little fuzzy on those details," said Trix. "But it seems that Trebald and Saturday were not the only ones to survive."

"There was someone else?"

Trix shrugged. "And a horse, apparently."

"But no other brownies." The firelight flickered against Lizinia's golden skin, sparkling and casting dark shadows at the same time. "How very sad."

Now it was Trix's turn to feel ungrateful. Of course if Trebald had been the only one to escape, then he'd lost his entire clan in the destruction of the Great Mountain. Trix couldn't imagine such a terrible thing. "A terrible thing," Trix murmured aloud. "Something terrible is always happening." As he spoke the words he felt the urge to douse the fire and run for Faerie as fast as his legs could carry him. What if the world ended while they were sleeping?

"Now, Trix, depressing yourself about the situation won't help Trebald. We must stay positive, for his sake."

Trix forced himself to remain calm. Mama always said it was better to face troubles after a good night's sleep, and that's exactly what he must do. "Those are the words I said to the Faerie Queen in the vision, when she made me her Emissary. Oh, Lizinia, the world is in danger, and it's up to me to save it."

"Saving the world. Goodness, that's an awful lot to ask of one young man."

"Something has bound the magic in Faerie. Those with fey magic can no longer work spells, and those with any animal magic have turned into animals. They're scared and running wild." Trix felt that sense of urgency crawl under his skin again as he spoke, and he ordered it to be still. "I have to speak for the animals."

"Still." Lizinia poked at the fire with one hand. The gold protected her from the flames, but she had to be careful not to touch anything directly afterward with a scalding palm. "Faerie is a *country...*"

"...and I am just one boy," Trix finished. He was beginning to feel more and more inadequate by the moment.

"Then it's a good thing I'll be along to help you," said Lizinia. "And your sister, too."

"My...Saturday?"

"Well, it just makes sense, if we'll be passing by the abbey anyway," said the golden girl. "That is where she'll be headed, I imagine, based on everything you told me before."

It seemed like ages since Trix had bespelled Mama and Papa and Peter and Saturday and fled the towerhouse. He'd been compelled by a vision of his birthmother—he'd be happy to never experience another vision again for as long as he lived—to make the journey to Rose Abbey all on his own. That was when the earth had broken. Saturday had somehow broken the world *because he had run away from home.*

Trix smacked himself in the forehead. What with all the questing for fathers and volunteering to save the world, he had almost forgotten. "Saturday is looking for me."

"It does make sense," said Lizinia. "I'm sure she will want to help us."

"Yes, yes," Trix said, adopting the brownie's speech pattern playfully. "Our odds will be far better with Saturday on our side."

He'd be much more comfortable with his invincible sister and her magical sword on hand. He'd have *complete* peace of mind if Wednesday and Aunt Joy were in fighting form...but if that were the case, the Faerie Queen wouldn't have needed to call upon him in the first place.

"There's just one thing we need to do first," said Trix. "I need a weapon."

Lizinia tilted her head to the other side. "You have your dagger."

"Exactly what I told the Faerie Queen," said Trix. "She did not feel it was enough."

"Rose Red might be able to find you something at the abbey. What sorts of weapons can you use?"

"I had a bow, briefly, as a boy." Thursday had given him the bow this past spring; he'd been a boy up until only a few weeks ago.

"The abbey employs hunters. I'm sure someone has an extra you can use."

"I suggested that too...sort of. The Faerie Queen said that wouldn't be enough. She told me to find a woman on an island. She can give me a bow that will be more effective against the beasts we'll be facing."

"But I thought you were summoned to make peace with the animals," said Lizinia. "I don't understand why you'd need a weapon."

Trix tried to sort it out, but his mind was quickly overwhelmed by that desperate need to get to Faerie as soon as possible. "If some are too far gone to communicate, that could be a problem."

Lizinia sighed. "You had to wait until all the water was gone to search for an island."

"Wasn't my idea. Besides"—he nodded to the sleeping

brownie—"the queen said he could help us."

"Then I suppose we should follow our guide's example and get some rest."

They banked the fire and laid down close to the embers. Trix's mind was racing, full of so many stories and questions that he was sure he'd never fall asleep. He closed his eyelids, desperate to try.

The next time he opened his eyes was when Trebald stuck his nose in one of them.

Trix shot up, surprised by the damp and uncomfortable greeting. It was morning, but just barely. Only a blush of pink on the horizon gave a hint that the sun would soon be making an appearance.

"Good morning, Giant-brother," Trebald replied. "Metal-girl says you need my help, yes? To find an island, yes?"

Trix stretched, scratched, and wiped the sleep from his eyes. Glad as he was that the brownie had not absconded in the night— brownies were nocturnal by nature—his dreamless sleep had been incredibly pleasant.

"Yes, yes," Trix said without meaning to. He accepted the piece of bread and chunk of cheese Lizinia passed to him.

"I took the liberty of updating Trebald on our own adventures," she said. "I told him that we are on our way to Faerie at the special request of the Queen, but that she specially requested that we stop and collect something for her along the way."

Trix smiled to himself as he chewed—Lizinia was too clever by half. She hadn't told Trebald everything, but there was no sense in troubling the brownie with the rest. Though she wouldn't have known it, that was the best way to converse with animals. Too much information sometimes led to confusion down the line. He made a mental note to commend her for her quick thinking…later, when he was far more awake.

"I told him all of this, but I'm not entirely sure he understood me," said the golden girl. "Back when I lived with the cats we would have conversations—they were mostly one-sided anyway, even with Papa Gatto."

Leave it to cats to make life difficult with as little effort as possible. It was a miracle that Lizinia had put up with them for as long as she did…no doubt the reason why Papa Gatto had rewarded her so greatly. Trix dropped his hand and stroked Trebald's fur. It was coarse, yet soft, and the thickness of it was beginning to shed. The days were growing colder, as usual with the turn of the seasons, but Trix imagined it was still warmer here than at the Top of the World.

"Yes, yes. Tell the metal-girl I understood her just fine," said Trebald. "I see why you travel with her, yes, yes. She makes a fine companion. Her belly rubs in particular are quite wonderful. Yes, yes."

Trix chuckled.

Lizinia waved a golden finger at them. "Now then, it's all fine and well that I can't hear the animals like you, Trix Woodcutter, but I'll not have you sharing jokes at my expense right under my nose."

Trix caught her hand and kissed the back of it playfully. "Trebald heard you just fine. He was commending your excellent belly rubs."

Lizinia took back her hand and covered her own smile with it.

"Oh. Well, he's very welcome." She turned to Trebald and said loudly, "*YOU'RE VERY WELCOME.*"

Trix winced a little. "He's blind, Lizinia. Not deaf."

"Sorry." The brownie accepted her apology by nosing his way back over to her and graciously accepting more belly rubs. "He reminds me of the kittens," she said. "He even purrs a little."

The colony of cats that had employed Lizinia was where felines lived out the last of their nine lives. Trix hadn't considered that there might be kittens among their numbers. He didn't want to think about what awful thing would have ended the nearly-immortal life of a kitten so soon.

"Trebald," said Trix, "the Faerie Queen said that you could help us find this island. Do you think you can?"

The brownie reluctantly turned out of the belly rub and brushed his whiskers. "Yes, yes. Have always been good at finding water, yes." He ambled off Lizinia's lap onto the ground, stuck his nose in the air, and turned a small circle. "No water here, though. No, no."

"Then we should start heading west. Are you ready?" Trix asked Lizinia.

The golden girl stooped and addressed Trebald in a normal tone of voice. "Might I have the honor of carrying you for a while, good sir?" The brownie answered by walking up Lizinia's arm and settling down in the curve of her neck, beneath the curtain of her golden hair.

Lizinia looked out into the forest, took a deep breath, and exhaled slowly. "The cats had a saying about how unlucky it is to retrace one's steps. I hope that's just a saying." She adjusted the pack on her shoulders, making sure Trebald was resting comfortably. "And I hope your Faerie Queen's not in a terrible hurry."

"I rather think she is." Trix felt the pull of the urgency in the pit of his stomach and tried not to dread how long it would take to acquire this mysterious bow. He fixed his eyes on a movement in the leaves, a shift in the dappled shadows of the sunrise, and he smiled. "Happily, I don't believe speed will be a problem."

3

The Great Stag

rix made a shushing sound and clicked his tongue against his teeth two times. Lizinia stayed very still, becoming a golden statue in the autumn-painted woods. The deer approached Trix cautiously.

"Hello there," he said softly. A fawn this young would not be without her mother. The last thing he wanted to do was spook her.

"Hello," the fawn answered, skittish, but still cheerful. "Are you lost?"

"Always," said Trix. "But today I have a direction. What about you? Are you lost?"

"What kind of mother would I be if I allowed that to happen?" The large, black-tailed doe emerged from the brush in her daughter's wake.

"One with a headstrong child." Trix bowed to the graceful beast. "Or so my own very good Mama says."

"Your Mama is a smart woman."

"She is a woman who had ten children, though only one as beautiful as your daughter."

This time, it was the doe who bowed. "You are kind, Boy Who Talks to Animals. Is there some way the deer can be of help to you in your quest?"

With the help of the deer, the journey time to Faerie would be cut in half. "My friends and I are traveling west, milady. To Faerie, on an errand for the Queen. I am to be her Emissary."

"Goodness," said the doe. "Faerie is awfully far from here. Even for the eagles."

Trix wondered if her choice of bird was coincidental. "Her feyest majesty has also tasked me with a side errand: to find a woman who lives on an island."

"The Spirit Sister." The doe named the woman as naturally as if she were speaking of her own sister.

"You know her?" said Trix.

"I know of her," said the doe. "But I have never met her."

"Her brother is a Great Spirit," the fawn added enthusiastically. "And her island is invisible! Daddy told me the stories. The Island of the Spirit Sister floats in the air. But in the morning when the mist is thick, or in the evenings when the clouds bend to kiss the trees, that's when the Spirit Sister comes to earth."

"Her father is quite the storyteller," said the doe.

Trix knelt to meet the fawn's eyes. "I have a Papa who tells stories, too."

"We can help you travel to Faerie," offered the doe, "but I'm afraid I don't know the location of the Spirit Sister's island."

Perfect. Trix's skin tingled in anticipation. He'd half a mind to hop on the doe and gallop straight to Faerie without stopping. But even if he skipped catching up with Saturday, the Queen had ordered him to fetch that infernal bow. "One of my friends believes he can find it," said Trix. "In the meantime, whatever speed you can lend us will be much appreciated."

"Who are your friends?" asked the fawn. "I don't see anyone. Just that shiny statue there."

"That's not a statue. That is Lizinia! Doesn't she have a marvelous disguise?"

"Hello," said Lizinia. The skittish fawn leapt away from her, and then slowly crept back as she spoke. "I'm so sorry. I didn't mean to frighten you. This is Trebald. His clever nose is going to find the island for us."

Upon hearing his name, Trebald emerged from beneath Lizinia's golden fall of hair and waddled down her arm to perch in her cupped hand. He wrapped his claws around Lizinia's fingers and nosed the air, whiskers atwitch. "Deer, yes? It has been a long time. There are deer in the Great Mountain, yes, but not at the Top of the World, no." He sniffed the air some more. "Young deer, yes. Very young. And very old. Yes, yes. Old as the sky and the land. Only one beast older I know, yes. Ran from it yesterday."

Trix eyed the doe, grateful that many beasts did not communicate between species. Having grown up beside a mother and many sisters, he knew women rarely enjoyed mention of their advanced age. This doe may have been an experienced mother, but she didn't seem particularly old to his eyes.

"It seems even I cannot hide from Sir Trebald's considerable talents."

The deep voice made Trix's bones hum. Trix saw the antlers first, the height and breadth of them almost as large as the animal himself. Glad that he was already kneeling, he bent his head low. Beside him, Lizinia took to one knee and lowered the brownie in her hand to the ground.

"Daddy!" The fawn pranced over to her father. Her tiny, spotted body danced around his regal form.

"Your Majesty," said Trix. "You honor us."

"I am likewise honored by the presence of the Boy Who Talks to Animals and his esteemed companions," said the Great Stag.

"I can hear him," Lizinia whispered in awe. "The words echo inside my head. It is...he is...magnificent."

"The Great Stag was born with the Wood and the Winds," Trix told her. "Or so says the legend Papa told me when I was his daughter's age."

"Your Papa was correct." The Stag's voice was strong and comfortable and dangerous. In many ways, it reminded Trix of Papa. "But then, Jack Woodcutter always was an eloquent man."

"You know my Papa, your majesty?" asked Trix.

"I have often found myself in the Elder Wood," answered the Stag. "I have made myself known to the men allowed to fell trees in that part of the Enchanted Forest. They are a rare breed—there have been but a handful in my time."

"I offered to aid them, my love," said the doe. "They are destined for Faerie, but they first seek the Spirit Sister."

"You mean to ask for her brother's bow," said the Stag. It was not a question.

"Yes, your majesty," answered Trix.

"I find myself reluctant to help you acquire a weapon of such magnitude. This weapon has been desired by many hunters, but only a few have been worthy enough to wield it. Do you think you are worthy, Trix Woodcutter?"

Worthiness, Trix had found, was never decided by the person being tested. "I am only one boy—one man—and I try my best. The Faerie Queen deemed me worthy enough to be her Emissary. It is up to this Spirit Sister to decide whether or not I am worthy enough for her brother's bow."

The Stag stepped forward, looming over Trix with his glorious presence. As much has Trix had grown over the past few weeks, he suddenly felt smaller than he had in a very long time. "You are a credit to your parents."

The Stag hadn't specified which parents, his birthparents or his foster parents. Trix supposed it didn't matter. "Thank you, your majesty."

"We will carry you to your destination, on one condition."

It didn't sound like Trix had much of a choice. "Yes, your majesty?"

"Whatever weapon the Spirit Sister gives you, you must promise not to hurt any living animal."

Trix and Lizinia (and Trebald, if he followed them that far) were about to descend beneath a Hill full of wild animals with wilder magic. How was he to defend himself if not with this bow? He had accepted the Faerie Queen's mission, so he had to fetch the bow, even though the Stag's provision rendered it mostly useless. The only other option was arriving in Faerie on foot, when it was too late to save the world from being torn apart from this magical imbalance.

Trix clenched his fists a few times, trying to shake the nagging feeling that they were already too late. It was the Stag's duty to protect the animals of the Wood. Trix could never fault the protector for doing what he'd been born to do. "Yes, your majesty. I promise."

"Then let us not delay. My wife will bear you. I will take your companion."

"Thank you, your majesty," said Lizinia.

"And what about me, Daddy? What can I do?" The fawn pranced about again, eager to help.

"What say you, Trebald," said Trix. "Would you like to have your own mount for this journey?"

"Yes, yes," said the brownie. "I think that would be a splendid idea."

"Tell him to be careful with those claws," said the fawn as Trix moved Trebald from Lizinia's hand to the fawn's back.

"Trebald will watch his claws," Trix said. "But he is sometimes a nervous traveler, so you must be careful not to jump around or go too fast and scare him."

"Yes, sir." The fawn held her head high and made sure to stand as still as she could.

Trix helped Lizinia up onto the back of the Great Stag, and then mounted the doe in one fluid leap. In his boyhood, he'd had a regular communion with such animals. He missed those days.

"You are a good man, Trix Woodcutter," the doe said to him as they turned away from the rising sun.

"As you say, milady," Trix answered. "I just hope I'm good enough."

It had been too long since he'd ridden with the deer. The brush of the wind through his hair, the burn of it on his cheeks. The beat of his heart increasing with the beat of the doe's hooves on the ground and then stopping—along with his breath—as they leapt impossibly high over rocks and creeks and fallen trees. His muscles seemed to melt into the doe's and they became one beast, flying over the landscape.

It seemed that the magical storm had left its mark on the forest. Typically, the dying leaves of autumn were red and gold and amber. However Saturday had disposed of the ocean and remade the earth, she had done so with the full spectrum of an artist's palette. Some trees boasted leaves of the richest umber, some were turquoise...one of the maples they passed was bedecked in shades of pink. Some trees had leaves like the Faerie Queen's eyes, running the gamut from blood red to indigo to intense violet.

Every time he closed his eyes, she came to him. *Save us, Trix Woodcutter. Save us all.* He had hoped not to be haunted by the queen as he'd been haunted by his mother's vision, the one that had compelled him to take his first adventure, but he hoped in vain. The memory of her kept coming back to him, along with her words, and the desperate need inside him to move onward, farther, faster, to reach their destination.

Judging by the periodic whoops and hollers from the backs of the other deer, Lizinia and Trebald were enjoying themselves as much as Trix. He'd been worried that the brownie's nervous nature would slow their pace, but it seemed that Trebald's dislike of heights did not extend to excessive speed. They sped past bushes and clearings and meadows filled with wildflowers that brought back his memory of the Faerie Queen again. They ran so fast that the trees became a blur, their jewel-toned leaves reminding Trix of the maelstrom, the colored sky, the rainbow lightning, and the dragon. Part of him wished he'd seen the dragon.

They did not find the Spirit Sister on the first day. They paused several times so that Trebald could give the area a thorough sniffing, but the brownie had yet to sense anything beyond a hint of water. A dry forest was a foreign thing to the son of a woodcutter. The Enchanted Wood where Trix had grown up was rife with randomly scattered Fairy Wells. As strange and sometimes threatening as their contents could be, he would never again take them for granted.

They spent the night in a small clearing abundant with mossy earth and mushrooms, but thankfully no fairy rings. Trix dreamt about the Faerie Queen anyway.

In the morning, they awoke to find their clothes and hair and skin and fur completely damp with dew.

"She was here," said the brownie. He had burrowed in the crook of Trix's arm for warmth. Lizinia made a great perch, but when she slept her metallic skin became as cool as the night. "Yes, yes. She was here."

"I agree with Sir Trebald," said the Stag. "This dew carries with it a hint of the old magics."

"The clouds came down from the sky and slept beside us," the fawn said in wonder.

"And we slept right through it," Trix said grumpily.

"I wonder why she didn't wake us," said Lizinia.

"Perhaps she meant only to make our measure," said the doe.

This thought did nothing to help Trix's disappointment. Had

the Spirit Sister found him wanting already? A cowardly act for a goddess, if she was a goddess. Trix should at least have had the chance to prove his worthiness to her face to face!

"Daddy, I'm tired," said the fawn. "And thirsty."

Trebald sniffed the air. "I sense no streams nearby."

"We can collect the dew while it's available," offered Lizinia.

Any other day, Trix would have felt compassion for the fawn, but he didn't want to delay any longer than they had to. The closer they got to Faerie, the more his soul would be at peace. "Do you think this dew is safe to drink, your majesty?" he asked the Stag. "You did mention magic."

"It is safe," said the Stag. "As long as you all remain by my side."

And so they spent precious time collecting dew from the largest leaves and blades of grass they could find. Lizinia refrained from drinking. Trix, too, did his best to quench his thirst only minimally, saving what water they had for their mounts and the brownie who was their guide. The noble gesture made for a good excuse—he did not relish the thought of drinking magical water, however powerful the Great Stag might be.

They set off again, ever and ever westward. They stopped as often as they had the previous day, for the fawn and the doe to rest, and there were fewer exclamations of joy from companions. The Stag never winded bearing Lizinia's golden form, but she appreciated the ability to dismount and stretch her legs. Her armor, it seems, did not preclude her from sore muscles and stiff joints. Trebald nosed about every time, as was his duty, and every time he found next to nothing.

That night, when they stopped to make camp, Lizinia and Trix collected firewood together.

"Gather all you can," said Trix. "I mean to stay up all night. If the Spirit Sister comes again, I will not miss her."

"I will join you," said Lizinia. "We can each help to keep the other awake."

"That will help," said Trix. "Thank you."

"I, too, am happy to stand watch," said the Stag.

"Rest with your family," said Trix. "You will need to bear us further tomorrow."

The Stag did not argue. He bowed his great head slightly, the strong muscles of his neck bearing the weight of those massive antlers with incredible ease. He moved a short distance from the fire and knelt down beside his wife and child. But Trix had the feeling the Stag would still keep a watchful eye, and he was glad of it.

4

The Spirit Sister

"I feel terrible," Lizinia said as she built the fire and lit the kindling. She'd made a bed out of her pack for Trebald, who had curled up inside it and fallen asleep immediately.

"Long days riding will do that, but your body will get used to it eventually."

Lizinia rubbed her legs—the sound of metal sliding against metal was strange, but not entirely unpleasant. "I'm not sure I could ever get used to this. But that's not what I meant. I feel terrible that we're troubling this family to carry us so far out of their way."

Trix shrugged. "They offered."

"I know," said Lizinia. "It's just…when I lived with my mother and sister, before the cats, nothing was done without the expectation of reciprocation. Every gesture of kindness came with a condition. The greater the gesture, the greater the repayment."

"You realize, that's not kindness."

"I know that now, yes."

"And after living with the cats for so long, you must know that animals do things very differently than humans."

Lizinia nodded and poked the fire with her foot. "I do. But there were still expectations. I had duties in the colony, and Papa Gatto oversaw the performance of those duties."

That wretched cat still oversaw all Lizinia's actions, even from beyond death. "The Stag is a legend in the Wood. Every animal is a friend. Every forest is his home. The offer he made to us was rare and special. I can assure you, he would not still be with us if he suddenly changed his mind, or had to deal with more pressing matters."

"Like a dragon," said Lizinia.

"Like a dragon," Trix agreed.

"Your sister Saturday sounds like she was a bit of a dragon herself."

"I believe she could give the beast a run for its money."

Lizinia's slight grin made Trix feel triumphant. It had been a long time since he'd talked the night through with Sunday, but the casual banter tripped off his tongue as if they'd done it only last week. Out of nowhere, he suddenly missed his beloved little sister most painfully. In many ways, Trix felt as if Lizinia had always been a part of his life, but in reality, it had only been a few short weeks...maybe even a full month now. The benefit to the newness of their friendship meant that they still had a plethora of personal stories to share.

Astute Lizinia read his body language all too well. "What is it?"

"You remind me of my sister," he said, not wanting to go into detail for fear he might lose his composure in this sudden grip of grief.

"The one that woke the dragon?" asked Lizinia. "Not that it matters—I'm sure that all of your sisters are far more pleasant than mine, so I take the comparison as a complement."

"The one who became a queen," he said.

"Even better." There was a snort in the silence, and Lizinia whipped her head around, listening into the trees. "What was that?"

Trix waited until he heard the noise again. And again. "I do believe Trebald is snoring."

The golden girl put a hand over her mouth to muffle the laughter.

Thanks to Lizinia's powers of conversation, the night turned out to feel far shorter than Trix had anticipated. Before he knew it, the heavens were already beginning to lighten in the east. They'd talked the fire to embers several times, watched the stars disappear and reappear behind rows of clouds that trekked across the sky. There had been no sign of the Spirit Woman or her legendary island. *Perhaps tomorrow*, thought Trix. He and Lizinia were listlessly comparing their worst winters ever when he began to feel drowsy. *A few minutes won't matter now*, thought Trix. *Sleep will put me in a better mood later, and my friends will thank me for it.* He closed his eyes once, twice, three times, letting himself relax to the cadence of Lizinia's golden voice.

PAIN.

"Ow!" he cried and put his finger to his lips. The brownie had bit him.

"She's here," whispered Trebald.

The clearing that had only a moment ago been filled with firelight and Lizinia's stories was now shrouded in a cloak of darkness and silence. Even the embers of the fire were black and cold. Trix tiptoed over to Lizinia's sleeping form and shook her shoulder to wake her. His hand slipped across her skin—everything was covered in a damp sheen of dew.

Trix put a finger to his lips when her eyes opened. Lizinia nodded, lifting Trebald to his spot on her shoulder. Behind them, in the darkness, the deer family continued on in their peaceful slumber. Before them, between their campsite and the ever-growing light in the east, was a mountain of cloud.

"What should we do?" asked Lizinia.

"Climb it," said Trix.

Slowly, together, they made their way toward the summit. The cloud mountain was as solid as any real mountain, able to hold Trix and Lizinia's combined weight with ease. There were cloud-rocks, cloud-trees, and cloud-paths that wound up and up and up. It all smelled like lightning and petrichor. The difficulty was not the incline—though it was steep enough—but that water covered everything. The mist that enveloped them made everything slippery. Water droplets beaded up and ran down Lizinia's gold. By the time they reached the top, even Trebald had been spattered with his fair share of cloud-mud.

Finally, when there was no more up to go, they found themselves standing before a great structure.

"I expected a palace," said Lizinia. "This looks more like the mouth of a cave."

"I see a light coming from somewhere inside," said Trix, "but I wouldn't know how to get there. Caves are often filled with pits and falls and dead ends.

"Lucky that one of us was born in a cave then, yes?" said Trebald. "Let me down. I will lead the way. Yes, yes. I will take us to the light."

Slowly, the three of them made their way deeper and deeper into the bowels of the massive cloud-cave. The walls shifted from cloud to ice to a mist that shone with its own inner light, so they were never wrapped in total darkness. They lost sight of Trebald a time or two, but the brownie sensed when they were falling behind. He would turn back to them, his blind eyes flashing yellow in the mist-light, before resuming his steady pace onward.

Once Trix began to shiver, he couldn't stop. He was jealous of Lizinia's imperviousness to the weather…and careful not to touch her golden hair or skin or clothes as the ice crystals spread across them. Not that she noticed. He tried to focus on anything else to warm himself—the Great Stag's request, the Faerie Queen's mission, the interrupted journey to the King of Eagles—but the cold seeped into him, bone deep, and did not let go.

The winding tunnel led them into a large room. Had he not just climbed a cloud-mountain and spelunked through a cave of mist, Trix would have thought he'd just stepped through the door of a hunting lodge. The mist beneath their feet mimicked planks of wood, complete with natural grain and whorls. There was an enormous fireplace that ran the length of a far wall that looked to be made of old stone. The flames inside flickered with colorful sparks, but it smelled like any other wood fire might, and the heat emanating from it was tremendously powerful...and welcome. Trebald scurried over to it immediately. Trix and Lizinia did the same, ridding themselves of the chill of the cloud-mist. Lizinia began to drip as the webs of ice crystals upon her melted.

"I would know the names of those who share my fire."

Trix turned to see the woman whose stern, gravelly voice had broken the silence. She stood beside a giant table surrounded by four thrones. This table, too, was made of solid, mistborn wood. The woman had long, black hair, a face weathered by too much sun, and a pale dress made completely of animal skin. The table hadn't been there when they'd crossed the room, nor had the woman, but they were there now.

"I am Trix Woodcutter." He purposefully omitted the names of his companions. Trix had learned from Papa that one only gave the most basic information when speaking to gods. It helped that he was still so racked with shudders that it made speaking a challenge.

"You have come to ask for my brother's bow." Every syllable was slow and precise, as if this tongue—or speaking in general— was not her common language.

"I have." Not that he could have nocked an arrow, or even held a bow, with ice-cramped fingers.

"Sit." The Sister gestured to the four thrones before her. "All of you."

The thrones were works of art. The one farthest from the fireplace, the tallest one, was made of fur and bone. A set of antlers large enough to rival those of the Great Stag rose up from the back. Across the table, closest to the fireplace, was a throne of sand and glass. It was all one piece, wound about itself in a deceptively delicate design. Each whorl was laced with silver and gold and tiny granules that sparkled like diamonds. To the right of the bone chair sat a lush throne of differently flowering vines that all sprang from the same cherry and purple wood. There was a sinuous figure carved at the top of the back, behind a few fat, white buds. Trix squinted in the firelight, and then smiled.

"Can you make it out?" Lizinia whispered to him.

"It's the lingworm," he answered.

The last throne was the least ostentatious. Solid wood like the table and floor, it was polished to a sheen and whittled full of intricate designs, figures, and runes. Trix ran his hand lovingly along the smooth back. For a moment, he could smell the bark and the grass, hear the wind in the leaves and Mama calling him home.

"Elder Wood," said Trix. "I would know it anywhere."

The Spirit Sister nodded slowly, and gestured for him to take his seat.

Trix slid himself into the Elder Wood throne. Lizinia likewise perched in the throne of glass, looking for all the world as if she'd been destined to sit there all her life. Trebald climbed up the vines of the living chair and sniffed about before chomping heartily on the colorful foliage. Trix tried to remain as stoic as the Spirit Sister as he watched and prayed they would not be thrown out on their collective ears for eating the furniture.

"What is this place?" Trix asked.

"The Hall of the Four Winds," said the Spirit Sister. "My brother is the Spirit known as the East Wind. You currently sit atop his throne."

Trix felt his eyes pop. This wasn't the home of just any old god, this was the Hall of the Four Winds! Elementals, reportedly the most ancient gods of record! He could not wait to tell Papa *this* story! Urgency surged beneath his skin once more.

Trix examined each chair with new eyes. The bone chair was undoubtedly for the North Wind, which made Lizinia's glass throne the seat of the South Wind. The exotic flowers and thorny vines must belong to the West. "I hope my choice is a good sign," said Trix.

The Spirit Sister gave no indication one way or the other. "Once a guest chooses a chair, he or she is drawn to it every time and will sit nowhere else."

The Hall of the Four Winds had frequent visitors? Perhaps it was easier to reach on subsequent visits. Did that mean he would be welcome here again? No doubt the Spirit Sister expected Trix to return her brother's bow when he was done with it...

Trix felt something poking into his back. He reached around to a split in the wood and pulled out an enormous black feather. "And this belongs to...?" Trix prompted. Couldn't be one of the Winds. Invisible spirits had no need for wings.

"Death," said the Sister matter-of-factly. "We always save the opposite chair for his wife, but Fate has yet to visit."

"No wings?" asked Lizinia.

"Exactly," replied the Sister.

Trix resisted the urge to leap straight out of his chair. Death had sat here? Death *always* sat here? How recent was his last visit? How long had that feather been lodged in that chair? Was Trix losing years of his life just by touching it? Trix instantly released the feather and it floated to the tabletop. The Spirit Sister picked it up and tied it into her hair, where it disappeared among her raven tresses.

"I will give you my brother's bow," the Sister said to Trix, "if you can tell me what it is made of."

Trix suddenly felt sick. A riddle. He hated riddles. He could rarely hold his concentration long enough to solve them. Almost every time he'd entered into a battle of wits with a magical animal in the Enchanted Wood, he'd bungled it royally and paid the price. The last time, he'd brayed like a donkey for a week.

He tried to think out the problem logically. This bow would have power in the land of Faerie, deep in the Enchanted Wood. The bow belonged to the East Wind. And the throne of the East Wind was made of...

"Elder Wood," Trix guessed confidently. "His bow is made of Elder Wood."

The Sister neither smiled nor frowned. "That is not the right answer."

"*What!?*" Trix couldn't stop the word from exiting his mouth. It had to be the right answer! Didn't the Sister know Trix was the luckiest boy in the world? Didn't she know he was on a quest of vital importance? When the shock of it wore off, Trix squeezed his eyes shut and balled his hands into fists. He was tired and hungry and frozen. He wanted to run about the room, screaming his frustration. They'd all come so far, only for him to fail. He had failed the Faerie Queen.

Save us, Trix Woodcutter. Save us all.

He felt Lizinia's hand slide over his, the metal of it now warm and smooth. "May I try?" she asked the Spirit Sister.

Trix wasn't sure he could handle failing the Faerie Queen twice. "Are you good at riddles?" he asked his companion.

Lizinia shot him a sideways glance. "I worked for cats."

The Spirit Sister ignored their banter. "State your name," she said in that same gruff monotone.

"I am Lizinia," the golden girl replied. When the Spirit Sister did not speak further, Lizinia added, "Of the Colony of Cats."

"Very well, Lizinia of the Cats." The sister nodded to Lizinia, her serious expression unchanged. "I will give you my brother's bow if you can tell me what it is made of."

Like Trix, Lizinia's approach to the riddle was logical. Unlike Trix, she spoke her thought process aloud. "A bow must be long and supple, so the material has to bend without breaking." She stood and moved to Trix's chair, examining its makeup as if it might provide her with some inspiration. "You are gods, so it must be something magic." She ran her golden fingers along the Elder Wood. "But you are more than gods. You are *Elemental* gods. Which means that it must be something natural...but also something wonderful."

Trix was about to add to Lizinia's thought process when something bit him. "Ow!" he cried, and instinctively put the injured finger in his mouth. Trebald curled himself around the carved arm of the Elder Wood chair and looked entirely too proud of himself. The brownie's expression reminded Trix far too much of Papa Gatto.

"If we get three chances, you'll be next," Trix said to the brownie with a mouthful of finger.

Trebald yawned. "I have faith."

Muttering to herself, Lizinia paced her way back to the fireplace. The flames there still flickered cheerfully in a myriad of colors. "Spirits are invisible, so it could be something invisible…but magic could easily make something invisible as well. At the very least, I couldn't imagine it would be something heavy. The bow would have to be light."

One of the logs in the fire chose that moment to split, falling to ash in a shower of colorful sparks. Trix looked to the Spirit Sister. Her hard expression had not changed…but she had raised an eyebrow.

Lizinia snapped her fingers, which sounded nothing like a snap at all. "*The bow would have to be light*," she repeated as she turned back to the table. "Mist and light and beautiful and natural and magical and sometimes invisible."

Trix furrowed his brow. Every word of the list she had just rattled off could have been used to describe Papa Gatto. Except that Trix would never have referred to Lizinia's godfather as "beautiful."

Lizinia placed her hands on the table across from the Spirit Sister. "Your brother's bow is a rain-bow."

The Spirit Sister…smiled. The expression changed her face from dour to beautiful. Trix suddenly felt a lot less frightened, and a lot more relieved.

"And what would you use for arrows?" asked the Sister.

"Something small and shiny and sharp…and also light." Lizinia's smile now matched the Sister's. "Stars."

"Well done!" The Spirit Sister rose from the throne of the North Wind with her arms spread wide. She embraced Lizinia, kissing the golden girl on both cheeks. Trix tried not to appear too shocked by this shift in demeanor——Papa had told countless stories about the whims of the gods. Trebald, full of faith and stuffed with magical flowers, began to snore.

"You remind me a little of my own sister," the Spirit Sister said to Lizinia. "She thought her skin a burden, but it was her clever mind that won my brother." She took Lizinia's hands in hers. "Of course, *he* was the one who forced her to take the test. I could see the purity of her heart in her eyes the moment we met. As I see it in yours."

Trix bristled. Had the Sister not seen purity in his heart as well? And could they please get the bow and go to Faerie now?

"Thank you." Lizinia was not used to being lavished with such affection. As jealous as Trix should have been that she'd outwitted him, he could not find it in himself to be envious.

The Spirit Sister walked to the mantle above the sprawling fireplace and reached into the mistwall. From it she withdrew a crystal bow that scattered hundreds of rainbows over the room as it caught the light from the fireplace. With it came a quiver of ebony arrows. The Sister slid one of them out to show that it was indeed tipped with a tiny, pointed star.

The Spirit Sister helped Lizinia with the straps of the quiver and showed her the best way to carry the bow. "You have been found worthy, Lizinia of the Cats. I would be honored to call you sister."

Lizinia looked as if she were about to cry, but no tears—of water or gold—escaped her eyes. "The honor is mine," she said, and the Sister embraced her once more.

The Spirit Sister turned to Trix and embraced him as well. "Thank you, Trix Woodcutter, for bringing me both a hero and a sister. I will cherish this day for a lifetime."

"I'm only sorry I wasn't your hero." Trix looked at Lizinia, whose smile still beamed from ear to ear. "But not that sorry."

"But I cannot allow you to leave empty-handed. Please, accept these with my gratitude." The Sister reached above the mantle again. This time she pulled from it a far more humble bow and a quiver of plain, wooden arrows. "There is no magic in this bow, but I suspect there is already enough magic in the young man who will use it."

"You may be right," he said. "Thank you."

"A sister knows," said the Spirit Sister. "Your own sister is looking for you. More than that, she needs you. And so I have delivered you to her."

"You've...delivered us?" asked Trix. "How?"

The Spirit Sister shrugged. "My brother is the East Wind. Blowing us westward cost him little effort. Your paths will cross here. Look for a wagon." With that, the room and the table and the cloud-mountain began to dissolve around them. Lizinia quickly scooped Trebald up off the Elder Wood throne before it disappeared completely.

"Goodbye, my sister," they heard the goddess call. "Goodbye, my friends. May the winds of good fortune blow ever at your back."

5

The Return of Saturday Woodcutter

he Hall of the Four Winds lifted like the fog it was, leaving Trix and his companions in a forest glen. It looked very much like every other forest glen they had passed through since leaving Rose Abbey, though the trees here boasted normal autumn colors, amplified with an amber hue from the setting sun. Trix wondered how much time had passed while they were in the company of the Spirit Sister. Gods had a way of affecting time as well as space.

"Do you see her?" asked Lizinia.

Trix grimaced into the tree line. No deer. No Saturday. No true idea where and when they were beyond the god's vague description. "Perhaps her path has not crossed ours yet."

"Time for lunch, then. Yes, yes." Trebald's voice sounded muffled—Trix and Lizinia looked down to see the brownie's hind legs and stub of a tail sticking out of one of the packs.

"At least the Sister was kind enough to deliver our things along with us," said Lizinia. "Wherever this may be."

Trix was glad to see their bags, though carrying them along with their bows and quivers would be a tad more complicated. Lizinia's mention of the Spirit Sister distracted Trix. He turned to his companion and put his hands on his hips. "So...does being the sister of a god make you a god now?"

She opened her mouth, closed it again, tilted her head to the left, and then to the right. "Godsister sounds more appropriate, doesn't it? More like a ceremonial thing. Sort of like Papa Gatto. His being my godfather doesn't make me a cat."

"Goddaughter and godsister." Trix shook his head slowly. "Quite the godfamily you have there. And a god's weapon, to boot! I don't know... Papa always said, if it walks like a god and sounds like a god..."

Gold scraped gold as Lizinia folded her arms across her chest. "If I am a god, does that mean I outrank you?"

Trix pretended to think about it. "Hmm. I'd say yes if I were just a prince, but I'm a prince *and* a prophecy."

"Equals, then?"

"Equals it is." Trix shook the hand Lizinia extended. "Why don't you stay here with Trebald. I'll scout around and see if I can find a road or path or an animal friend who can lead us to a road or a path." He'd also look for something else to eat, since Trebald seemed to be finishing off what little they had left.

Lizinia smirked. "You want to try out your new bow."

"Well..." Trix had learned from Mama that deception was no

longer useful once caught. "Okay, yes. That too. But I hope you'll wait for me before you try out yours."

"I will," she said. "Though I may have you give me a few lessons with yours first. I don't want to hurt anyone."

"Deal," said Trix, and he moved deeper into the forest.

He jogged out a ways, looking for signs of...anything. He found a patch or two of edible greens—including those dandelions Lizinia didn't care for—but they did little to sate his hunger. Not long after, he stumbled across some thick bushes with a few ripe berries left unpicked, which did more. It was still autumn then, and the colorful leaves weren't just stained with leftover magic. He just wasn't sure if it was the same autumn, or an autumn a hundred years from when they'd left. Of course, if they'd been in the Hall of the Four Winds for a hundred years with fey magic still trapped under the Hill, there probably wouldn't have been a world to come back to...never mind a world with berry bushes.

Save us, Trix Woodcutter. Save us all.

The urgency of the Faerie Queen's plea pushed him onward.

He marked his way through the forest with arrows. He worked on his pull and his stance and the angle of his elbow, so as not to bruise his forearm bloody with string slap. The bow felt good in his hands; the touch of Elder Wood was like home. *This* was the bow he would have chosen if he'd had the will of a god: carved from the most powerful trees of his home, as well as anything Peter might be able to fashion with his magic knife. But even without god magic (or the correct answer to the riddle), the Sister had still given him the bow his heart had longed for.

Oh, the whims of the gods.

Trix had no godmother or nameday gift himself, but he did have seven very powerful sisters, and now a boon from a god. The lingworm had said—it felt like ages ago now—that the prophecy that had named him had been around before the gods became gods. Trix had teased Lizinia back in the clearing, but he now wondered in honest just exactly how one became a god. Not that he'd ever want the job.

"I say, your accuracy could use some improvement."

Trix spun around once, twice, trying to find the source of the voice. The third time, he saw the tortoise hidden in the pile of dried leaves.

"Good day to you, sir," said Trix. "Might you be able to tell me where I am? In human terms?" Trix learned long ago to specify—animals often gave directions that included landmarks only animals could see. Or smell. Or hear.

"North and west of Rose Abbey," the tortoise replied slowly. "I believe that is the closest human-hole." Human-holes were houses, villages, inns, hovels, or anything else an animal didn't have a word for.

"I am looking for my sister. Can you tell me, have you seen her?"

"Can't say that I have," said the tortoise with great condescension. "What does she look like?"

Trix thought back to Trebald's incredibly accurate—if slightly unkind—description. "Like an angry, fair-haired giant."

"Sorry," said the tortoise. "No giants here. You must travel even farther west for that."

Farther west. To Faerie. He really needed to find Saturday, and soon.

"Thank you just the same," said Trix. He collected his arrows and moved on. He found another sizable tree and nocked his arrow...but then relaxed when he noticed two sparrows on a low branch there.

"Hello," Trix greeted the birds. "I am looking for my sister. Can you tell me, have you seen her?"

"No humans, no humans," twittered the birds.

"Save you," chirped the first. "Save you."

"Slightly human," chirped the second.

"Terrible archer," chirped the first.

"Gee, thanks," said Trix. Birds were known for their gossip. Trix wished fewer people trusted their skewed versions of the truth.

The wind picked up and the birds lifted their wings.

"Save us," chirped the first as it fluttered away.

"Save us all," chirped the second.

Trix wasn't entirely sure if he had heard the birds correctly—echoes of the Faerie Queen's vision had been swimming unceasingly around his head since he'd seen her. He sent two arrows into the trunk of the tree to his left: one high, one low. The third did not have enough force behind it—it simply hit the tree and fell to the ground.

"I'd find another line of work if I were you," said a squirrel.

"My arm is tired," said Trix. "I'm actually looking for my sister. Have you seen her?"

"Are you going to shoot her?"

"Not at first. But she can be a bit surly."

"Mmm," said the squirrel. "I have a sister like that."

"Is there a path through these woods? Maybe something that runs westward to Faerie? My sister would be on a road like that."

"If she is, may the gods help her," said the squirrel. "There's a wolf on that path. No mistaking that smell, no sir."

Saturday was strong enough to hold her own, but one wolf usually meant a pack of wolves, and the Spirit Sister had said that Saturday needed him. Everyone needed him lately, it seemed. "Which direction?"

"That way," pointed the squirrel. "But I wouldn't go there. No sir, not for all the nuts in the world."

"Thank yooooou!" Trix called behind him as he sped into the forest.

He stumbled across the path so quickly that he almost couldn't stop. It had two bare lines, well worn from wheeled conveyances. Had the forest been cleared for better passage, it might even be called a road. But the fey were particular about their foliage, so any "road" running into Faerie would eventually become so increasingly dense as to be unpassable.

It was difficult for Trix to get his bearings in the twilight. Fireflies began to rise up, darting in and out of the bushes. Which way? He closed his eyes and called once more on that dormant animal part of him, daring himself to detect that scent of wolf on the wind. Other than the chill in the air and the sweat from his running, he smelled nothing. Saturday would either come upon him at any moment, or she had already passed him. How was he supposed to know which?

And then suddenly the air was filled with cursing more colorful than the Spirit Sister's fire.

"Saturday," Trix said beneath his breath and took off at a run. The voices grew louder as he approached and he slowed his pace.

"I could run you through right now." Saturday sounded angry. Furious, even. She was definitely talking to someone.

"I wish you'd wait," said the someone. A male someone. His voice was deep and soft, as if this someone possessed infinite patience. Anyone traveling with Saturday would need infinite patience.

There were more words, even softer. Trix stayed just out of sight and forced himself to be as still as possible while he strained to make out the conversation. The last sentence ended with, "You love me."

Please, Trix scoffed in his mind. *Saturday doesn't love men, she clobbers them with swords.*

"You loved me first," said Saturday.

"No *way*." Trix spoke before he could stop himself. Well, that had done it. Surely he had given himself away. After a moment of silence, Trix poked his head out of the foliage. Saturday and her someone were now hugging. Tightly.

And that will be enough of that, he thought to himself before stepping out of his hiding place and applauding. They certainly couldn't miss him now.

Saturday stepped out of the embrace, but the someone didn't let her go far. Had she been…crying? No. Couldn't be. Saturday Woodcutter did a lot of things, but she did not cry. And if this someone had made her cry, then Trix would just shoot him with one of his arrows. He'd only promised the Stag that he wouldn't shoot animals.

She looked taller, his giant sister, as if that were possible. Then again, he'd gotten taller too, according to Lizinia. The long, bright blonde hair that had always fallen in a plait down her back was gone now in favor of a shorter style—cropped close to the nape and slightly longer than chin-length in the front. It suited her.

He did not have to run to her, for she'd already swept him up in a bear hug worthy of Papa. The bowstring bit hard into his breastbone and the strap of the quiver cut into his neck, but he didn't care. He did, however, care about the giant sword in her hand. She might be invincible, but he wasn't.

"Watch it, sister."

Saturday backed away, apologizing. As soon as she'd sheathed her sword Trix caught her up in a hug, kissing both cheeks. After all the trouble he'd put her through, there was nothing she needed to apologize for. And she *had* been crying.

Saturday's companion introduced himself as Peregrine. He was taller than Trix, but shorter than Saturday, and had a better sense of fashion than both of them put together. He was the spitting image of a tribesmen of the north from Papa's stories, apart from the elf shot in his black hair. The streak almost looked blue in the fading light.

"I'm Trix," he said as they shook hands. "The one who got her into this mess."

"I fell in love with your sister in the middle of this mess," Peregrine replied.

"We both have stories to tell," said Saturday. There was a faraway look in her eye.

Peregrine took her hand. "I just hope you're better at telling stories than your sister," he said to Trix.

In one move and one sentence, Peregrine had managed to convey just how much he really knew about Saturday. Trix's warrior sister was not one to shun affection, but she did not seek it out. Nor did she draw attention to it; if Trix hadn't seen Peregrine take her hand, he might never have noticed.

Peregrine also seemed to possess intimate knowledge of his sister's atrocious storytelling. In a family of tale swappers , Saturday Woodcutter was tone deaf. At some time—perhaps even multiple times—Saturday had been at ease around Peregrine long enough to string more than ten words together.

And he'd made fun of her! Saturday took a ribbing as well as she could parry a direct attack—those who sought to bait her did well to prepare themselves for the subsequent thrashing. Peregrine stood beside Saturday and goaded her without fear.

One move. Once sentence. To a brother, they spoke volumes. Trix suddenly held the odd fellow in much higher esteem.

"How did you find us?" asked Saturday. "Aunt Rose's animals told her you'd turned back to Faerie. We left the Abbey to find *you*."

That's right…if she'd just seen Rose Red, then… "You know about Mama."

"I know." Saturday looked at her feet, a move she always made when she felt guilty about something. "If that witch hadn't stolen me away, I might have been able to save her from Aunt Sorrow's horrible sleeping spell."

"Or you might be asleep too," said Trix. "Oh! And did you get to meet Jack?"

Saturday cracked a smile at the mention of their long-lost, back-from-the-dead, legend of an eldest brother. "I met Jack," she said. "And my fist would love to meet him again."

Trix laughed at that—punching Jack was exactly something Saturday would do. He told her the abbreviated version of meeting Trebald, and the brownie's description of her as the bad-tempered giant in a skirt. "Then again, maybe he meant you. Trix nodded to Peregrine's double-breasted coat with burgundy piping. It flared out around the knees; instead of trousers beneath it, he wore hose. "If I were a blind brownie, I might guess that was a skirt," he said. "Goodness knows I've worn my share a time or two. Price of growing up with sisters."

Talk of Trebald reminded him of the companions he'd left behind in the forest. Now that he'd found Saturday, they could all get on with the mission. "We need your help, Saturday. The Queen of Faerie has named me her Emissary."

"Now I'm worried," said Saturday. "The Faerie Queen must be desperate indeed to have made such a choice."

Before Papa Gatto's aging spell Trix would have kicked Saturday in the leg for that remark, but he was a young man now. His sister should thank her lucky shins. "She asked me to speak to the animals. And for the animals."

"So the animals are in trouble?"

"Yes," said Trix. "All the animals in Faerie, and the Queen, and Wednesday, and Aunt Joy, and...well...pretty much everybody in the whole world."

"Again?" asked Peregrine.

Saturday smiled. Yes, there was definitely a story there. No matter who told the tale, Trix looked forward to it because it contained dragons. "You in?" she asked Peregrine.

"Always," he answered, his voice dripping with smoochiness.

Trix resisted the urge to step between Saturday and this man-in-the-skirt, if only in order to prevent further delays.

"Same here," said a third voice.

From the bushes stepped the most magnificent creature Trix had ever laid eyes on. No horse of his acquaintance had ever been so blindingly white. Nor did any of them possess wings. Oh, such enormous wings!

"Saturday," Trix said reverently. "You have a *pegasus*."

Saturday patted the withers of the pegasus. "Trixie, dear, I have a lot of new surprises."

"As do I," Trix replied. "I'm traveling with companions as well. I should go fetch them. We can be off at dawn."

"No need," said a lower, gruffer voice. "We can collect them on the way. Sassy won't mind pulling the cart through the night."

Trix caught the flash of yellow eyes. He'd been so stymied by the presence of the pegasus—he still was—that he hadn't noticed this man lurking in the shadows. He wore a wide-brimmed hat and a large coat, but neither were enough to conceal the fact that this was not a man at all. This was a wolf. A wolf that walked and talked like a man. No wonder the squirrel had warned him away. Even without his animal sense, Trix was wise enough to be very, very afraid.

"Are you the King of Wolves?" asked Trix.

The wolf's laugh sounded like gravel and thunder. "Gods, no. Do I look like an Animal King?" The wolf narrowed his yellow eyes. "How many Animal Kings have you met?"

"Just the two," said Trix. "Well...unless you count the Great Stag.

Would he count? I don't suppose it would make sense to have a separate King of Deer. And I know the cats don't have Kings, but if they did, I'd nominate Papa Gatto. He's certainly powerful enough. And then there were the gods. Well...the sister of a god. And maybe another one too, but I only heard her voice in a vision. And the Queen of Faerie, of course. But that was another vision. Are we counting visions?"

The wolf said nothing.

This time it was Peregrine's turn to laugh. "And you think *Saturday* is bad at telling stories."

"Enough." Saturday was either too tired or too emotional to be having any of their nonsense right now. Trix guessed the latter. "Betwixt can take Trix and me ahead to collect his companions. We'll meet up with the cart further down the road."

"And then to Faerie," said the wolf.

"With all due haste," said Trix.

The wolf pulled on the brim of his hat and sank back into the shadows.

Peregrine grabbed Saturday's elbow before she could mount. "One quick thing," he said to her. And then to Trix, "Do you mind?"

"Not at all," said Trix as Peregrine pulled Saturday out of sight.

"Those two have a lot to work out," said the pegasus.

"I wish them luck," said Trix. "I'm not sure anyone has ever 'worked things out' with Saturday in her life."

"You do know your sister well," said the pegasus.

"As do you, it seems," said Trix. "How is that exactly?"

"A witch was holding us all prisoner in a cave high in the White Mountains."

The Top of the World, Trix guessed. Trebald's home. "So you woke a dragon and destroyed the mountain to escape."

"And killed the witch, too." The pegasus pawed at the ground, then bent to nibble some grass there. "Storytelling is a lot less fun when the audience already knows the ending."

Trix shrugged. "I still don't know the details. Like how a pegasus and a dragon exist in this world when both are supposedly extinct...for instance."

"The dragon was put under a sleeping spell and frozen in time," said the pegasus. "But you're right about the pegasi. They don't exist. I'm a chimera."

Chimeras weren't supposed to exist either, but Trix refrained from mentioning this to his new friend. "A chimera named Betwixt. That's very clever."

Betwixt blew out his lips in a long sigh, a sound horses often made when either pleased or bored. "It's the only name I can remember."

Before Trix could ask more about Betwixt's mysterious name and the exact nature of chimera, the breeze brought them the sound of Saturday's laugh, followed by Peregrine's shout.

"They'll be about done now," said Betwixt. "You ready?"

Trix mounted the pegasus, making sure not to ruffle the enormous feathers on his way up, and then scooted back to make room for Saturday. Saturday emerged from the trees with Peregrine hot on her heels. He helped her up, but instead of saying goodbye, he looked her dead in the eye and said, "You owe me an explanation."

"Fight me for it," said Saturday. "Let's go."

"Where's your sword?" Trix asked as Betwixt walked them to a less dense path of woods.

He felt her muscles tense in front of him. "Do I need it?"

"No," said Trix. At least, he hoped not. And then he hoped for nothing more in the world as Betwixt bent his hind legs, spread his wings, and flew. Trix held onto Saturday tightly, hooting and hollering as Betwixt soared and dipped. The crisp wind stung his cheeks and made his eyes water, like riding a deer without ever touching the ground. Beneath his grip, he could feel Saturday laughing.

It didn't take them long to find Lizinia in the dark of the night. She had started a small fire, small enough that it might have gone unnoticed had it not been for the reflection of the flames off her shiny gold skin. Trix pointed, but Betwixt had already spotted her and started his descent.

Trix kept his eye on Lizinia as the pegasus dropped from the sky to land before her. She jumped up from her seat beside the fire in surprise and then kept jumping, clapping with excited glee.

"Your companion is a girl entirely made of gold," Saturday muttered as Betwixt settled. Though she said nothing else, the tone of her statement made fun of Trix in every way possible.

"Your companion is a man who makes you cry," Trix responded in the same tone.

Their eyes met as they dismounted, and between them they called a silent truce.

"Saturday, this is Lizinia." Before Trix had even finished his introduction, Lizinia had launched a hug at Saturday from a running start. Saturday, giantess that she was, caught her with ease, but still had to take a step back from the force of her gesture. "Just like Friday, eh?" he said to his sister.

"Uncannily," said Saturday. "It's lovely to meet you, Lizinia."

"Trix has told me so much about you," said Lizinia. "About all of his sisters. Forgive me for getting carried away...it's just, I feel like I know you."

"I look forward to knowing more about you too." Saturday eyed Trix, silently scolding him for not preparing her at all for this meeting. "This is Betwixt, my pegasus-for-now."

Lizinia cocked her head. "Pegasus-for-now?"

"Until I decide to be something else," said Betwixt. "But changing takes an awful lot of effort, so it's pegasus for the time being."

Lizinia curtseyed to the chimera as if she were being received by royalty. "It's an honor, Betwixt."

Saturday continued to examine Lizinia. Trix recognized the expression; it was the same one Saturday used when trying to size up an opponent. "Now she reminds me of Sunday."

"Didn't you say 'companions,' plural?" asked Betwixt. "I don't see anyone else here."

"I'll fetch him!" Lizinia said perkily. "You were gone a long time," she whispered to Trix. "It made Trebald nervous. He's eaten almost all the food."

"We'll be fine." Trix went with her to retrieve the packs, both of which were considerably lighter than they had been before. Lizinia scooped up Trebald. Together they put out the fire.

As they walked back to Saturday and Betwixt, Lizinia held out her cupped hands, which cradled the brownie inside. "This is Trebald," she announced.

"You!" Saturday shouted at the brownie. "You have got to be kidding me," she said to Trix.

Betwixt snorted and whinnied.

"What?" said Trix.

"You told me you had spoken to that idiot brownie, not that you were *traveling with him.*"

"Sorry," said Trix. He loved his sister, but he knew how hotheaded she could be. Defiantly, he stuck up for his friend. "Trebald's help has been invaluable to us. We wouldn't have made it this far without him. What happened between you?"

Trebald trembled in Lizinia's hands. "Don't want to talk about it, no, no."

"I'll tell you what happened," said Saturday. "In a moment of...*compassion*"—she spat out the word—"I saved that wretched brownie's hide. And how did he repay me for it? Did he thank me? No." Saturday brandished the index finger of her right hand. "He *bit* me!"

The tip of Saturday's finger boasted an angry red gash that didn't look to be healing well at all. Trix stared at it in horror.

His sister was no longer invincible.

6

The Spriggan

ou're a better shot than me," Trix said as he retrieved Lizinia's arrows for the tenth time that day.

Thankfully, teaching Lizinia what little he knew about archery distracted from Trix's jumpiness every time the adventuring party stopped to rest. What with the addition of a pegasus and a wagon to the party they'd made good time, so Trix couldn't complain, but he still couldn't shake the pressing need to be at the Faerie Queen's side.

The urgency seemed to grow stronger the closer they got to the Hill. Like the previous visions of his birthmother, Trix saw the Faerie Queen in his mind every time he closed his eyes to sleep, and that first moment every morning before he opened them to wake. Her glowing violet eyes bore into his very soul.

Save us, Trix Woodcutter. Save us all.

They hadn't stopped much, only as needed for food and stretching and the swapping of steeds. Only Wolf never gave up his role as wagon driver. Despite his human appearance, Wolf had far more animal in him than fey. Even if he could endure riding, no beast would have been comfortable bearing Wolf as a burden. It was a wonder that Old Sassy tolerated Wolf as well as she did, but Trix knew some bonds of friendship could never be explained. Or broken. Whatever the reason, the mare trotted along, happy and unfazed.

Wolf had been the one to kindly point out exactly how little Trix knew about bows and arrows. He'd stood before Trix, coarse hand outstretched. His yellow eyes bored into Trix's soul, and there was the faintest hint of a growl on his breath. Trix had simply handed over the bow and stepped back.

Wolf used Trix's bow to demonstrate how Lizinia should hold the rain-bow, how and how far she should pull back the string. Ever eager to learn, Trix went through the motions beside them empty-handed, practicing the stance Wolf instructed, drawing his crooked finger back to his chin every time. Wolf's stance didn't seem so very different from his own...until Wolf gave him the bow back. Trix loosed an arrow and the bowstring slapped the inside of his arm on the first try. Trix cried out from the burning pain of the welt on his already tender forearm. Saturday and Wolf had little sympathy.

It was Peregrine who wrapped a spare shirt around Trix's arm. "You need a proper bracer, but this should do for now. Don't let those bullies get to you," he said, indicating Wolf and Saturday. "They're all bark and no bite."

Peregrine meant well, but Trix had seen Saturday swing that sword, and Wolf's wicked teeth had not gone unnoticed. Regardless of how much barking either of them did, those two had serious bite.

Lizinia practiced with the rain-bow, but Wolf decided to leave the star arrows in their quiver, since no one was quite sure what sort of magical havoc they were meant to wreak. He started Lizinia on Trix's arrows instead. She had no need for bracers, what with being covered in gold and all, and she hit the target on the very first try. From that point on, she'd only gotten better.

"It must be magic," Lizinia said with great humility. "The only things I've ever been good at are cleaning house and tending cats."

"And talking to gods. And wearing golden armor. And blinding people in direct sunlight. And..."

"All this shooting off at the mouth." Wolf's voice was so close behind Trix that he nearly jumped out of his skin. "You want to shoot something, shoot that tree. Ten more times each, and then we're back on the road."

They passed no stream before twilight, so Betwixt took to the skies with Saturday and Peregrine to find the nearest source of water. After much coaxing, Trix convinced Wolf to let him be the one to unhitch Old Sassy and rub her down. Sassy was as old as her name implied, and she talked more than Grinny Tram after three pints of honey mead.

"Sassy isn't my real horse-name," she'd said when Trix first introduced himself. "Humans and fey give names to us domestic types, but only because we can't tell them our true names. Which is a shame, really, since true names are usually much lovelier and far more original. You wouldn't know it to look at some of us, but horses can have the wildest imaginations. My horse-name is Falada. Isn't that beautiful? It was my grand-mare's name."

"Very beautiful," said Trix. "Well met, Falada. Would you like me to tell Wolf your true horse-name?"

"Goodness, no. You don't need to make no nevermind," said Sassy. "Heaven knows Wolf wouldn't like it one bit. Wolves don't take to kindly to change."

"How well do you know Wolf?" he asked casually. Trix knew that Wolf met up with Saturday and Peregrine at Rose Abbey, but he knew nothing more about the man-beast himself. Unlike Old Sassy, Wolf wasn't particularly chatty.

"Know that fool better than his own britches, I'd say. Been with him nigh on…my goodness, it's been so long. Would you believe I've lost count? He and your Uncle Bear have been best friends since I was knee-high to a spriggan. We always thought that would be a double wedding. Shows how smart we were…and how vicious Fate can be."

Sassy spoke with such enthusiasm that the conversation lost Trix before she paused to take her first breath. "What's a spriggan?" he asked.

"Guardians of Faerie," said Sassy. "There are a slew of great stones framing the entrance to the Hill, on either side. Those stones are the spriggans, ghosts of giants who roam the Wood looking for miscreants. Sometimes they take the form of men. Sometimes they take the form of the giants they once were. Sometimes they are shadows. Sometimes they are the stones themselves. They are *always* ugly. Even when they are stones. So ugly that the grass beneath their feet withers and dies with every step they take."

Trix wasn't sure he'd ever come across an ugly stone. He'd have to pay more attention in future. "The spriggans keep unwanted beings out of Faerie?"

"You know the old rag about humans and fairies and the balance of power?" Trix nodded. It was a tidbit Papa frequently included in his stories. There always had to be as many humans inside the borders of Faerie as there were fairies in the human world, to maintain a balance of power. If that balance shifted—if a particularly powerful fairy passed either way through the gates unannounced, or if a powerful spell was cast or broken—massive storms would break out all over the world, just to get the gods' attention. "Spriggans maintain that. As enforcers. They're also in charge of changelings and whatnot—they're fairly good thieves, what with their being ghosts and all." Sassy sighed and whuffled. "They do their best, poor dears, what with all the nonsense that's been going on lately." She eyed Trix with her big, brown horse's eye. "Mostly caused by your family."

"Sorry?" Trix didn't know what else to say.

"Not your fault, poor chicken. You're just the next in line to be brought in to right the wrongs. You aren't the first, and you won't be the last."

What Sassy said made him feel a little less special, but it was nice for something not to be his fault for a change. "And what was that about a double wedding?"

"Well now." Sassy chomped down on a healthy patch of grass before going on, whetting Trix's appetite for her next bit of gossip. It was too bad Papa couldn't hear animals the way Trix did. Trix suspected that Papa would like Old Sassy very much. "As you know, your Uncle Bear is married to your Auntie Snow White."

"Yes," said Trix.

"...and your Auntie Snow White and your Auntie Rose Red are twins..."

"Named after the rose bushes on either side of Grandma Mouton's front stoop," Trix confirmed.

"...and your Uncle Bear and Wolf have been best friends their whole lives..."

Trix slapped himself in the forehead for not putting it all together the first time, which gave Sassy quite the chuckle. "I completely missed that."

"So did Wolf," said Sassy. "He had his chance with Rose Red, but his stubbornness—and hers, might I add—are the reason she left and moved halfway across the countryside. Didn't stop him from losing his heart to her, though, and wolves only fall in love once. It's why he is the way he is."

"Growly and surly and ready to bite someone's head off at a moment's notice?" Trix guessed.

"Humanish," said Sassy. "Wolves like him, the enchanted kind, have the ability to change into human form during the full moon. Always been that way, always will be. Until a wolf like that falls in love. Then his shape takes after that of his beloved. And his beloved is human."

Human and fey, technically, but both were far more human in appearance than animals. "So he's in love with Rose Red, and always will be, and she *knows* it, because now he's trapped in half-wolf, half-human form. But neither one of them will do anything about it?"

"That's about the size of it, clever boy."

"Wow." Trix shook his head. "I suppose I'd be growly too."

Armed with this new information, Trix did his best to treat Wolf with more kindness upon returning Old Sassy to the wagon. A difficult prospect, as Wolf seemed even more cross than ever. For the life of him Trix couldn't understand why, because they were well into the Enchanted Wood now.

"Welcome to my home," Trix said to Lizinia. These were his trees, his soil, his animal friends. No matter where he had been born, the Enchanted Wood was where he'd been discovered and taken in by the Woodcutter family, and where he'd spent all of his growing-up years. The air smelled better. The birds sounded happier. Even the ground beneath the wagon's wheels felt more forgiving.

"Magnificent," Lizinia breathed.

"It smells divine," Trebald chimed in from his perch on Lizinia's shoulder.

Trix was pleased by their reverent expressions. "To me there is not a more perfect place in the world."

"I agree," said Saturday as she and Betwixt rode up beside them. "But I'm a great deal more comfortable on the days when the magic of the world is in balance.

If they traveled without incident, by tonight they would be on the border of Faerie. They'd arrive at the Hill—the high seat of the Faerie Court—by the next morning. At which point Trix and his small army could ride in and save the world. The Faerie Queen would be so pleased!

The deeper they drove into the Wood, the thicker the trees

became. Bushes began crowding the path, making the road almost impassible in some areas. Twice, they had to work together to pull fallen trees out of the way so that the wagon could cross. Eventually, it felt as if they spent more time clearing the path for the wagon instead of riding in it at all.

"This couldn't have been the way you came," Saturday called to Wolf as she and Peregrine hacked at branches with their swords.

"This is the main road through Faerie," said Wolf. "Leads straight to the Hill."

"It's the magic already," Trix said quietly. "It has to be." If fey magic had been used to keep the road clear, then its sudden impassability made more sense.

Finally, they managed to break through the worst of it. The road led on to a forest of tall trees and stones, with little brush or grass to speak of. Peregrine mounted Betwixt, while Saturday hopped into the wagon beside Trix and Lizinia, but neither of them sheathed their swords. As much as the Wood felt like home, the sense of something sinister remained in the air. Trix kept his bow to hand. Lizinia noticed and did the same.

"How funny would it be if Peter walked by," said Saturday. "Or Papa."

Trix had been thinking very much along the same lines. Before enchanted frogs and giant kings and the splitting of the world, Papa, Saturday, and Peter had gone into the Wood every day to work. Trix wondered if Papa and Peter still kept up the routine. "How far away do you think home is?"

Saturday answered without taking her eyes off the trees around them. "Maybe a day south?"

"Do you think they hate me?"

He'd been burning to ask Saturday the question since they'd met back up again, but he'd been afraid of her answer. Saturday was not one to pull punches, literally or figuratively.

"Mama called you a fool," she said after a few steps.

"Mama calls us all fools," said Trix. Mama's fey power was that every word she spoke came true. "Luckily, there are more ways than one to be a fool."

"They understood why you'd gone, though not why you felt you needed to do it alone." Saturday fiddled with the pommel of her sword. "Keep in mind, I'd just broken the world and there was an ocean lapping up on our back stoop, so we had bigger things to worry about. Like pies."

Trix's attempt to hold back his laughter made him burst into a guffaw. "Pies?"

"Mama took one look at the backyard and started fretting about the chickens, the fruit trees, and the barn, all of which were underwater."

"And no fruit trees means no pies," said Trix.

"She was actually thankful that you'd sold the cow this past spring. For all the good it did."

Trix selling that cow had set an incredible sequence of events in motion that might have ended very differently if Fate hadn't intervened. The most important part, however, was that none of his family was angry at him for running away. "Thank you."

Saturday must not have heard him, for she kept on. "And then Thursday showed up in her ship to take Mama and Erik and me to Rose Abbey, so we were all sort of busy with that. Mama got seasick right away. Did you know Thursday has seven men on her ship, all named Simon? I didn't really get to know any of them because the witch's bird snatched me up not long after that. I was glad to see that Erik was okay. He arrived at the abbey with Thursday. She cheered when I punched Jack. Put a nice dent in his that legendary lantern jaw *and* his pride."

Trix narrowed his eyes at his sister. She was mistelling the story on purpose, just to goad him. Saturday knew he'd give his right arm to have spent a day on the deck of a pirate ship. "You're such a *pest*," he said.

"I am the *best*," she rhymed, and punched him in the arm playfully. Thanks to his bigger frame, Trix was able to experience the punch without being knocked sideways, which was a first.

If Saturday noticed, she didn't comment on it. "I keep looking for somewhere—anywhere—that Papa and Peter and I have worked before," she said. "Gods know we've been all over this Wood."

"You don't recognize anything?"

Saturday shook her head. "Not that it means much. The Wood can erase the footsteps of a human in an evening. In a fortnight, you'd never have known anyone was there to begin with."

"Then I hope we don't lose our way," said Trix.

"We'll be fine," said Saturday. "Woodcutters have tricks. Breadcrumbs. Stones. Things like that."

"Do you happen to have any stones on you?"

Saturday paused, listened to the wind in the leaves for a moment, and then resumed talking. "I do, actually. Remember the three fairy stones Papa gave Sunday?"

He did, and the memory made him smile. Papa had come home from work and told Sunday all about a leprechaun he'd trapped in the woods that day, and the three gold coins the leprechaun had given him as payment for setting him free. How disappointed Mama had been when the fool's gold had turned out to be fairy stones…if it had ever been gold in the first place. Not that it mattered. To Trix and his siblings, Papa's stories were priceless.

Saturday reached into in her pack and retrieved the stones: one hazy pink, one green and mossy, and one blue shot with veins of white. "Take one. For luck. Lizinia too."

"Thank you," said Lizinia as she chose the pink stone.

Trix took the green. "It feels right to leave you the one that looks like waves on the deep ocean."

Saturday dropped the blue stone back in her pack, then ruffled his hair for good measure. While she had him close, she whispered, "Trix, I'm worried about Wolf. Have you noticed anything…strange about him?"

"Like, the deeper we get into the Wood, the surlier he gets? It's been a long journey for all of us, and I don't know him very well, but Sassy says he's a good man. I'm inclined to trust her."

"What else did Sassy say?"

"He has history with Rose Red."

Saturday nodded. "I know. I mean, I don't know the whole story, but I figured out the important bit. It's just… Something feels wrong."

Trix wasn't sure about his animal instinct, or even his fey instinct this close to Faerie, but his human self was definitely on edge. "I feel it too."

Fireflies rose up into the Wood after sunset, like stars blossomed from the earth. From beside Trix, Lizinia sighed. "I don't think I will ever tire of that sight."

"I never have," said Trix. Trouble was, other than the fireflies, he hadn't noticed a wild animal in the Wood for a very long time. They were a large party and made a fair amount of noise, so it wasn't too odd, but odd enough to make Trix extra attentive.

Right about the same time, the wagon began thumping oddly and took on a terrible wobble.

"Busted wheel," growled Wolf. He pulled Sassy into a halt and jumped down from his seat to examine the far side of the wagon.

"Maybe we should make camp for the night," Saturday said warily.

Trix nodded. Old Sassy began to prance restlessly, but she hadn't said anything to Trix.

"I'll set her loose." Saturday walked to the hitch, fiddled with it a while, and then cursed like a Simon. "This is impossible. These straps are old as grave dirt, Wolf. Why on earth do you still use them? Peregrine, hand me your dagger. I'm just going to cut her free." Saturday held out a hand and waited. And waited.

"My dagger is gone," Peregrine said finally.

"You lost your dagger?" Saturday asked with exasperation.

"Of course not," said Peregrine. "I..." But it seemed he didn't have a better explanation. He began retracing his steps down the path. Betwixt helped him.

Lizinia hopped down from the back of the wagon and joined Trix. "Something is wrong," he whispered to her. He didn't want to alarm everyone if there was no cause for it.

"Trebald is shaking like a leaf," she whispered back. "Something is off. And I swear I keep seeing movement in the shadows. Not fireflies."

There was a resounding *crack* and Old Sassy hopped away from the body of the wagon.

Peregrine, still searching for his missing dagger, called out, "Saturday, did you just use your sword on that strap?"

"No," Saturday said calmly. Too calmly. "The wood of the hitch just rotted away. Peregrine, you and Betwixt should come back. Trix, why don't you and Lizinia come up here with me?"

Trebald sniffed at the uneasiness in the air. "I don't like this."

"Wolf!" Saturday whisper-yelled, but if he heard her from the other side of the wagon, he didn't respond.

"I'm scared," Lizinia said, almost inaudibly. In moments, the small group was huddled together before the wagon. The waxing moon cast the shadows of the Wood sharply across the road, both the way they were going and the way they had come. Apart from his companions' heavy breathing, the road remained silent. Even the fireflies had moved on to safer paths.

Shadows. Thievery. Broken wheels and rotten hitches. Fear. Too much of what was happening reminded Trix of a conversation he'd had earlier. "Sassy," he whispered, "would spriggans hurt us?"

"I suppose they could," said the horse, "but I've never known them to. Mostly they're just mischievous."

"What are spriggans?" asked Saturday.

"The stone giant Guardians of Faerie," said Trix. "But they're only the ghosts of giants. Sassy says they normally only steal things and play tricks on people."

"The magic of the world is out of balance." Saturday raised her sword. "Nothing is *normal* right now."

Betwixt had ideas about that. "If fey magic tethered the spriggans' spirits to their stones like it kept the road clear..."

Peregrine held his sword high. "...then we are in big trouble."

"Trix," said Lizinia, "do spriggans look like bumpy evil shadow blobs with warts all over?"

"Sassy said they were so ugly that grass dies beneath their feet."

He looked down as he said it. They all did. Even in the darkness they could tell that the grass beyond their small circle was brown and dead.

"That qualifies," said Saturday. A monstrous dark shape rose out of the shadows and headed straight for Lizinia. Saturday swung her sword but it passed right through its body, as if it there'd been nothing there at all. Lizinia screamed as the spriggan touched her— a black spot appeared on her sleeve.

"You get away from her!" Trix yelled at the spriggan. Betwixt reared up as if to strike the spriggan with his impressive hooves, but the spriggan had already melted back into the shadows.

"Our weapons are useless!" cried Saturday. "What do we do?"

"I'm not strong enough to fly everyone out of here," said Betwixt.

"Peregrine, go," ordered Saturday. "Take Lizinia."

"I am not leaving you," Peregrine said adamantly.

"Nor me," said Lizinia, but her words were strained.

Trix was too busy worrying about his golden companion to argue. The attack had brought her to her knees. "Are you all right?" he asked.

"Tremendous…pain." The discovery of the right word to describe what she was feeling seemed to shock her. The expression on her face scared Trix worse than the spriggan. "I have not felt such pain in a very long time. Am I going to die now?"

He examined the dark spot without touching it. It didn't seem to be spreading. "No," he said with complete uncertainty. "You are not going to die. I bet a bit of cantaloupe will clear that right up. Can you hold your bow?"

"Trix," she whispered to him as he helped her stand and handed her the rain-bow, "are you positive I'm not dying? Papa Gatto's ghost is haunting that tree over there, smiling wistfully, as if he knows I'll be joining him soon."

Trix followed her gaze. Sure enough, that blasted incorporeal cat was staring down upon them from his perch in the nearest tree, but Trix saw no wistful smile upon the spectre. It looked more like the cat was scowling, at him particularly, and with much disappointment.

"Is that a—" Before Saturday could finish asking the question, Papa Gatto leapt from his perch. Saturday swung her sword again, to no avail. The sword passed through the cat just as the cat itself passed through the center of Trix's body.

Trix felt no impact, but the air left his lungs and his skin tingled. There was a damp spot on his shirt, right in the middle of his chest, marking the path of the ghostly feline. Trix laid his hand over it. It was not water, he realized, but frost. Beneath the cloth of the frozen shirt he felt the lump of Wisdom's tooth beneath his palm. He wished he knew what question to ask it to get them out of this mess.

As if he had said the words aloud, the tooth lit up like a star. Trix pulled the cord around his neck and lifted the tooth high above his head. The magic light illuminated the road and the trees of the Wood around them, revealing every spriggan hiding in the shadows.

"Dear Gods," breathed Saturday.

They were completely surrounded. Silhouettes rose up from the ground and hung down from thick branches. Some were smoky and insubstantial like Papa Gatto. Those that were more opaque had more sense of form, as if a shadow had come to life and grown arms and legs and...rocks. Their mouths were rocks. Their teeth were rocks. Their fingers were rocks. The rocks that made up their faces had depressions, but there were no eyes. Like Trebald, they didn't need to see.

The tallest, bumpiest form shuffled in the direction of the group, crunching the blackened grass beneath substantial feet. The ground beneath them appeared scorched.

"I smell death," whispered Trebald.

The spriggan turned its blind face to the sound of the brownie's voice and groaned, the loud keening of a corpse risen from the grave. The other spriggans answered the call. They began closing in as well, their footsteps becoming audible as they shifted from shadow into flesh.

Trebald scurried up Lizinia's arm and hid in the relative safety of her hair.

Trix held his breath. He didn't know what to do. If Saturday's magic sword had been useless, his arrows would have made no difference, goddess-given or not. He pulled the golden dagger from his belt. The lingworm had blessed the dagger with its blood and told Trix it would cut anything. He might be able to take down one spriggan, assuming it did any damage at all. Whichever form came closest to Lizinia would die before he touched her. And then Trix and Saturday and their friends would all perish at the hands of the rest.

He wished he'd been able to see the towerhouse one last time.

Lizinia, it seemed, had a different idea. As quietly as she could, she drew one of the star arrows from her quiver and nocked it in her bow. She pulled back the string, aimed for the closest spriggan, and loosed it.

The arrow lodged itself in the spriggan's chest.

The spriggan kept moving.

"Trix, you and Lizinia get on Sassy," Peregrine said as he leapt up onto Betwixt's back. "Saturday and I will hold them off long enough for you to get away."

Betwixt nudged Saturday in the back with his nose, but Saturday pushed him away. "Go. I've got this."

"I. Am. Not. Leaving. You." Peregrine repeated, with even more defiance than the first time.

Trix held a hand out to his golden companion. "Lizinia, come on!"

Lizinia aimed and shot another arrow into the spriggan. And another. The star-heads disappeared inside its shadow-rock torso, but they did not slow it down.

The urgency to leave was so strong inside him now that Trix felt ready to burst. "Lizinia!" he cried.

And then the spriggan exploded.

The stars from the arrow heads shot out of its belly in different directions, each heading for a different spriggan. The stars sank into the shadows and exploded into more stars, again and again until every single one of the spriggans had dissolved into nothing.

Trix and Saturday and Peregrine yelled cheers at the golden girl. Betwixt reared up on his hind legs and whinnied mightily in appreciation. Lizinia stood silently, staring into the space where the closest spriggan had been. The sparkling explosions drifted to the ground like drunken fireflies and the light began to fade.

"I didn't know…" she started.

She did not finish because the wolf had leapt from the shadows and clamped its jaws around her throat.

7

The Leprechaun

aturday threw her body upon that of the wolf, knocking it backward off Lizinia's prone form. Its teeth slid ineffectually across Lizinia's golden neck, and Trix thanked the cats for their ridiculous favors.

Saturday put herself between Lizinia and the wolf, sword raised. Unlike ghost giants, this beast could be harmed just as easily as any other. Trix had a clear shot with his bow. He aimed, pulled back the string...and remembered what the Stag had said.

Whatever weapon the Spirit Sister gives you, you must promise not to hurt any living animal.

Trix clenched his jaw as he looked down the arrow's shaft to the wolf beyond: its beady yellow eyes, its sharp bared teeth, the curl of its nose as it snarled, the drool as it growled. Wild fur stuck out all over its body, gray and brown and red and blond and...

Trix lowered the bow. "It's Wolf."

"What?" Saturday yelled as the animal lunged at her again. She dodged the attack, but once she was out of the way, the wolf made a move for Lizinia again. Saturday pulled the wolf's tail. When it spun around, she smacked it in the haunches with the flat of her blade. This made the wolf back up a few paces, but it did not stop his attack. Nor did it make him any less angry.

"We must be close to the Hill," said Betwixt. "The fey magic has drained from him and left the wild animal magic behind."

This time, it was Saturday who growled. "FINE. I won't kill him. But someone has to stay here and hold him off. For the last time, all of you, *get out of here*."

Instead of arguing with her again, Peregrine rolled his eyes to Trix. "Do you think Sassy could carry Lizinia?"

Trix didn't know Old Sassy's exact age, but he did know exactly how much of a burden all of Lizinia's gold could be. "No," he said truthfully.

"The pain has subsided," Lizinia told him. "I can run."

"Then run," said Peregrine. "Betwixt and I will help Her Royal Stubbornness drive Wolf in the opposite direction. Once we subdue him, we'll meet you at the Hill."

The attacks were coming faster now. Wolf had given up on the golden girl as a target and now seemed to be eyeing Sassy's neck. The horse neighed and stomped nervously. Saturday held Wolf back with her sword, meeting every one of his growls with a growl of her own.

"But..." Trix started, but he knew Saturday could handle herself, and the Faerie Queen needed him.

"Go!" yelled Peregrine.

Bows in hand, Trix and Lizinia turned away from the ruined wagon and did as Peregrine bade. Clouds rolled in and hid the moon, but it didn't matter. Wisdom's tooth lit enough of the forest around them with its pale light, and Trix felt the pull of the Faerie Queen like elfrope wrapped around his heart. To him, the direction was clear.

"He's gone," Trix heard Lizinia cry as they ran. "He's *gone*."

"He is not gone," said Trix. "We will fix the magic. And we will fix Wolf."

They ran in silence after that, not stopping until they came upon a stream. It did not occur to Trix that he was thirsty until he saw water. Together they fell to their hands and knees on the bank.

"Is it safe to drink?" Lizinia asked between gasping breaths.

"We're about to find out," Trix said, scooping up a handful of water and drinking deeply.

Trebald nosed his way out from beneath Lizinia's hair and hopped the short distance to the ground, careful not to touch the black spot on her sleeve where the spriggan had touched her. The dark circle seemed to suck up the tooth's magic light.

After the brownie slaked his thirst, Trix expected him to inquire about the status of their food stores. There was so little left in their packs that Trix had combined the contents into one, which he still carried, for all the good it did them. His stomach growled, half with hunger and half with the need to keep moving.

But Trebald did not mention food. Instead, he hung his nose to the ground. His notched ear drooped forward. "I'm sorry," he said to Lizinia. "I didn't know Wolf as well as you, but he was your teacher, and he taught you well. Take pride in that, and remember him any time you use that skill."

Lizinia patted Trebald gently with a golden hand. "I liked him," was all she said.

Trix was just beginning to like Wolf too, abrasiveness and gruff manner and all. It had taken Trix longer than it should have for him to realize how much Wolf was like Mama Woodcutter: stern, but kind. Wolf most likely pushed people away on purpose, to protect them from the brute force of which he was apparently capable. Much like Mama. In fact if things had gone differently—if his Aunt Rose Red hadn't been more stubborn than Saturday—Wolf could have been his uncle.

Save us, Trix Woodcutter. Save us all.

Trix shook his head. If they hurried up and got to the Hill, Wolf could yet be part of the Woodcutter family. "We can't talk about him that way. I can fix this. We can fix this."

Lizinia nodded.

Trix was a little jealous of her perfect stoicism. She didn't weep. She didn't look tired or thirsty. She didn't break a sweat, or smell bad. As heavy as he knew that gold was, she'd kept up with him the whole way. Her labored breathing was the only thing that gave her away. And when she lifted Trebald back to her shoulder, her golden hand trembled a bit.

"Are you all right?" Trix asked calmly.

"I'm fine," she said.

Trix had sisters. She was not fine in the slightest.

Lizinia touched the rain-bow she'd set on the bank beside her, and then pulled her knees in to her chest. "I killed the spriggans,

Trix. I killed them all."

Save us, Trix Woodcutter. Save us all.

The cadence of her words brought back the Faerie Queen's vision-chant louder than ever, but he forced himself to concentrate on Lizinia. Trix put one of his hands over hers and waited until her amber eyes met his. "The spriggans were ghosts, Lizinia. You can't kill a ghost. I dare say you put them to rest. And you saved us."

Lizinia stared at her knees. "I'm worried about Sassy. Wolf is her friend. Was her friend." She looked back up at Trix again. "*Is* her friend."

"What happened to Wolf is exactly the problem we're trying to solve," said Trix. "We just need to get to the Hill and find the Faerie Queen." He helped Lizinia to her feet and handed her the rain-bow. Trix turned a small circle until he felt the Faerie Queen's pull again, and then took a step.

"I wouldn't go that way if I were you," said a voice.

Trix's hand dropped to the golden dagger at his belt. Trebald slipped beneath Lizinia's hair once more. Lizinia had the rain-bow drawn and ready in the space of a breath. Wolf *had* taught her well. "Who's there?" she called into the shadows beyond the tooth's magic light.

"Victkor's the name. My friends call me Vick." From the underbrush emerged a man so small that his head came up only to Trix's waist. He had a cropped white beard and long white hair that flew about his head in a wild halo, but he did not look particularly aged. The hooded shirt he wore had been white at one time, and a small hammer hung at his belt.

Trix had never before encountered a leprechaun in person, but he'd heard accounts from Papa and the animals. Leprechauns were known for hoarding gold and causing trouble. They were also known for their long white beards. Perhaps this leprechaun had decided to be more fashionable. In a dirty shirt.

Leprechauns were *not* known for having friends. "Vick" held his hands up, palms outward, to show they were empty. Lizinia did not drop her bow.

"I have friends here," said Lizinia. "I do not count you among them."

"Friends?" the leprechaun said curiously. "The boy and...?"

"My bow," said Lizinia. Trix silently complimented her quick thinking. Leprechauns couldn't be trusted even when the magic of the world was in balance. There was no need to announce Trebald's hiding spot and play their hand all at once.

"And a fine bow it is," said Vick. "Well, as lovely as it's been to meet you, Miss Archer. If you'll excuse me, I'm just going to continue getting as far away from the Faerie Hill as possible. I suggest you do the same. Toodle-oo!"

Trix reached out with his own bow and hooked the leprechaun's hood before he could scamper off. "It's the middle of the night," said Trix. "Do you think traveling is wise?"

"Wiser than staying in Faerie one more minute? Yes," said the leprechaun. "Have fun at the Hill."

But Trix hadn't yet released him. "What's at the Hill?" asked Lizinia.

"Death. Destruction. Chaos. Savagery. Claws and teeth and blood. Fun for the whole family! Bring a picnic. Sneak in the secret entrance and you might live for a whole ten minutes longer." The leprechaun reached back to unhook himself from Trix's bow and then tugged at a stray white forelock. "Good evening."

Trix hopped around to block Vick's path.

"We need to know about this secret entrance," said Trix.

The leprechaun scowled at him. He turned to the left and walked straight into Lizinia.

"It's of dire importance," she said pleasantly.

Vick bared his teeth at her and growled. Compared to the ferocity of Wolf at full animal strength, the effect was almost laughable. Thankfully, Lizinia had the good sense to look surprised, if not actually afraid. The leprechaun spun on one foot, feinted left, and then jogged right, just as Trix had anticipated. He stuck out his foot and the overeager leprechaun fell sprawling to the ground.

The leprechaun pushed himself to a sitting position, spitting dirt from his mouth and wiping his face with his less-than clean sleeve. His eyes shot daggers, a move that paled in comparison to...pretty much everyone of Trix's acquaintance. "If I tell you, will you *get out of my way?*"

Trix grinned with great enthusiasm. "Most definitely."

The leprechaun took a great deal of time collecting himself. He stood and brushed the soil—some real and some imagined—from his clothing. He patted all of his pockets, checked the security of the hammer at his belt, and patted his pockets again. He smoothed his hair one way, and then the other. He pulled at his short beard, as if the act itself might make it longer. He looked from Trix to Lizinia, and then back again. Finally, he shook his head.

"You seem like such a nice boy. And a girl entirely made out of gold! Tsk. What a waste."

"I'm Trix," said Trix. "This is Lizinia."

"Dead Meat and Hunk of Junk. Got it."

"That's not what he said," said Lizinia.

"If I lead you into that Zoo of Death, it won't matter now, will it? Please. Come with me. Save yourselves."

"But we have to save Faerie," said Lizinia.

Vick threw his hands up in the air. "Says who?"

Trix folded his arms across his chest. "Says the Faerie Queen."

The leprechaun rolled his eyes and muttered something about no-good raven-haired magic-meddlers, women, and timing, but Trix couldn't quite make sense of it all. "Okay. So if you're facing the main entrance to the Hill—you can't miss it, it's framed by large rocks——"

"The spriggans," said Trix.

Vick eyed him sideways. "Yes. Them. Face the spriggans and head"—he waved his arm as if he couldn't think of the direction—"left. You'll want to go a ways…"

"'A ways?'" asked Trix.

"These directions don't seem incredibly helpful," said Lizinia.

"Look here, goldenrod, the way out's a lot more recognizable than the way in, or it wouldn't be very secret now, would it?"

Trix stomach growled with hunger and impatience, a measure of degrees louder than the leprechaun's feeble attempt. Vick was too close now for his bow to be of any use, so Trix brandished his dagger instead. "*Enough.* Her name is *Lizinia.*"

"I'll be sure to tell the engraver of her headstone. Hey, that is a nice dagger. Would you be willing to sell it? I've got a shiny gold coin with your name on it."

"Why would you trade gold for gold?" asked Lizinia.

"I'm about to give him a shiny black eye," said Trix.

"Stay calm, Trix. We only have to put up with him for a few minutes longer."

"A few minutes…or as long as I let him live." Trix didn't have the first clue what had gotten into him. He seemed to be channeling Saturday…and he liked it. Even better, the leprechaun was starting to look nervous. His bulbous nose twitched, but his lips remained a tight line beneath that white beard. The scamp wasn't ready to give in yet.

As Trix and the leprechaun stood there, locked in their battle of wills, a second round of fireflies began to rise from the grass and emerge from the trees around them. They brought with them a low, soothing buzz. Lizinia stretched a hand out to touch one.

"Er…you don't want to touch that."

Lizinia snatched her hand back and gave Vick a sideways look. "Why not? They're just fireflies."

"Those aren't fireflies," said Vick. "Those are spunkies. Bumble bugs."

"Fireflies are bugs too," Lizinia pointed out.

"A rag doll for the clever girl," sneered the leprechaun. "Trouble is, sweetheart, these bugs bite."

Trix was familiar with many of the bugs in the Wood, poisonous and otherwise, but he was beginning to realize that the Wood in Faerie was in many ways drastically different from the Wood he'd known all his life. It was hard to believe these bumble bugs could do harm to anyone. They looked so peaceful, floating about as if they had no particular place to go.

Trix leaned in as close as he dared without touching. The bumble bugs were more like wisps than insects, with no uniform body shape, nor any arms or legs to speak of. They did have wings, though, and teeth, shining like rows of needles by the light of their brethren. He quickly leaned away from the bug, rethinking his stance on the bumble bugs' capacity for damage. "Are they poisonous?" he asked.

"They're only poisonous if you're allergic to death or misfortune," said Vick. "And as much as you hated the thought of following me a moment ago, I strongly suggest that you walk in this direction now, slowly. Any faster and they'll sense your heartbeat on the wind."

Trix and Lizinia exchanged glances before obediently followed the leprechaun, moving deeper into the Wood. Lizinia's foot snagged on a fallen branch but Trix caught her before she plummeted headfirst into a cloud of cheerfully lit death and misfortune. As she caught herself, they hear a distinctive crunch. A foul stench filled the air.

"Oops." Lizinia lifted her golden shoe. Smashed against her sole was the glowing remains of a bumble bug.

"That's done it." Vick unceremoniously grabbed Lizinia's foot and used a leaf to remove what he could of the dead bug without touching it. "They'll be coming for the dead one now. The smell will draw them. I suggest we move along. Quickly."

Trix turned to see the luminescent cloud of bugs drifting toward them. "How quickly?"

"A brisk walk," said Vick. His considerably shorter legs had to work twice as hard to match Trix and Lizinia's pace, but he had no trouble keeping up. Nor did the bumble bugs.

"Or perhaps a nice jog," said the leprechaun, and they began to move faster through the trees. The bumble bugs stayed behind them.

And so they ran.

Wisdom's tooth continued to shine, and so they continued to follow the leprechaun, Though whether Wisdom was supporting their guide or simply the act of not running in the darkness, Trix couldn't decide. When there was no more stench and no more evidence of the bumble bugs, Vick stopped.

"We can part ways here," he said breathlessly. "The Hill is that way." He pointed into the trees beyond.

Trix knew from the pull of the Faerie Queen that the leprechaun was telling the truth. "Much obliged,"

"I'm headed this way." He pointed in the opposite direction. "Last chance to wise up and join me."

"Last chance to be brave and come with us instead," said Trix.

"It's for a good cause," Lizinia added.

"I wouldn't go back to the Hill if you paid me," said the leprechaun. "Not even for that shiny, incredibly well-crafted dagger."

Trix had no intention of offering the cowardly little man anything, but he raised his eyebrows as if considering the bargain.

"Help!" Saturday cried from the forest.

"Lizinia, did you hear that?" asked Trix.

"Help!" she cried again.

"Saturday's in trouble," said Lizinia.

"Oh you have got to be kidding me," said the leprechaun.

Trix ignored the small man. "This is not good. Saturday would never call for help unless she was desperate."

"You're right," said Lizinia. "We need a plan."

"Are you two hearing yourselves right now?" asked Vick.

"You stay here with Vick and I'll go check it out," Trix said to Lizinia.

"Stay here?" Lizinia shook her bow at him. "I'm the one who can actually hit something she's aiming at. Besides, the call is coming from this direction." She began to drift away from them both.

The leprechaun, tired of being ignored, walked over to Trix and stomped on his foot.

"Ow! Why did you do that?" yelled Trix.

Vick pointed at Lizinia. "Because I suspect it would have hurt me more if I did it to the girl with metal shoes. Now. Are you paying attention?"

Trix hopped, taking his weight off the bad foot. He'd been foggy-headed with exhaustion and hunger, but the pain and anger cleared that up a bit. "Lizinia and I need to get to the Faerie Queen. My sister and the rest of our party were supposed to meet us at the Hill. But there was a wolf—"

"Oh no." Lizinia gasped. "What if Wolf hurt her? Trix, we never should have left them."

"Help!" Saturday cried again.

"Save us!" cried the Faerie Queen.

"You must have heard *that*," said Trix. "I told you the queen needed our help. Now will you let us…what do you think you're doing?" The leprechaun had lifted his leg, ready to stop on the other foot. Trix pushed him away.

"That's not your sister," said Vick, "or the Faerie Queen, or anyone else you know."

Trix growled at the little man. For all his posturing about leaving them on their own, Vick didn't seem to be *actually leaving*. Trix was ready to see the backside of this pest. "I should think I know what my sister sounds like." Goodness knows he'd had the Faerie Queen's words bouncing around in his brain for so long that he'd recognize her voice anywhere.

"You said it yourself that she wouldn't be calling for help."

"Help!" cried another voice, this one deeper.

"Peregrine!" said Lizinia. "Or Betwixt! Oh, Trix, we must go to them!"

"You don't even know who's calling to you!" Vick yelled at them.

"Help!" yelled Saturday. She sounded closer. Or farther away.

Why were they wasting anymore time here? "Shouldn't you be on your merry way already?" asked Trix. "Good day to you, sir. Or good evening. Whichever you prefer."

"IT'S A FETCH," Vick growled, loud enough to cut through the panicked fog in Trix's head. "Don't you know what a fetch is?"

Trix stomped deeper into the Wood. "All I know is that my sister needs help. And after I help her, then I need to save the world. I am not as selfish as you."

This time the leprechaun tripped *him*. When Trix fell to the ground, Vick hopped on his chest and put a hand on either side of Trix's face, covering his ears.

"Trix, right?" Vick yelled into his face. His breath smelled like stale crackers and brine. "Trust me. The thing calling to you is a creature called a fetch. Probably more than one—they tend to run in packs. They lure innocent travelers such as yourselves into the forest in the dark of night by mimicking the voice of a loved one. And then they eat your soul."

Trix tried to shake off the leprechaun. "At least I have a soul."

Vick snatched up the end of Trix's bow and hooked his arm through it. "I can't let you do this."

"So we die by the hand of the fetch or the Zoo of Death, as you call it. What do you care?"

"Help!" cried Saturday.

"Hurry!" cried Peregrine. Or Betwixt. Their voices sounded closer.

"Get out of the way," Lizinia grabbed Vick's hood and lifted the little man off of Trix.

"Save us," cried the Faerie Queen.

"Help us!" No, *that* was definitely Betwixt.

"All right! All right! I'll take you to the Hill! I'll take you to the blasted Hill and prove to you that your sister is just fine."

It was a bold enough statement that Trix believed it, but Lizinia looked skeptical. "And Peregrine too?"

"And Grubwort and Pigsbreath and everyone else your sister happens to be traveling with, *yes*. We will go to the hill and meet up with your party and you will see that there is no one in this Wood who needs help." Vick smirked. "Present company excluded."

"Help!" cried Saturday.

Lizinia stared off into the Wood.

"Resist it," said Vick. "You must."

"What are we supposed to do?" asked Trix.

"Stop up your ears any way you can," Vick said. "Do you have anything in your bag that can start a fire? That will help keep them away. That magical doodad around your neck certainly doesn't seem to be helping."

As if offended, the tooth's light went out completely. Trix slid the mostly-empty pack off his back and rummaged inside it, looking for the flint.

"Help!" cried Peregrine. Trix steeled himself against the voices. He concentrated on his hunger. On the meager pile of sticks and leaves Vick shoved in front of him. On creating a spark large enough to coax a flame.

"They sound even closer now," whispered Lizinia.

"You'll want to hurry with that fire," said Vick.

The fire wasn't catching on the fresh grass. Too bad they hadn't stayed in the dead spot on the road where the spriggans had stepped.

"Help!" cried Saturday. She sounded almost on top of them.

"Save us," cried the Faerie Queen. But that was all she said. She did not say his name. She did not say the rest of the words. Trix concentrated on that difference as he struck the flint again and again.

Vick stopped tossing sticks on the pile and stood. He tilted his head from side to side, as if listening. Lizinia made a move to speak again, but the leprechaun raised a finger and she remained silent. Then he moved his lips, but no words came out. From deep in the Wood, they heard another cry.

Trix dropped the flint and covered his ears. All the voices—

inside his head, outside his head—and none of them real. He wondered if this was what it felt like to go mad.

"Oh, Trix, we have to help them!" said Lizinia. Only...it wasn't Lizinia. It was Lizinia's voice, but Lizinia hadn't said a word. She shrugged and pointed to Vick. Trix dropped his hands and listened closely, his eyes never leaving the leprechaun.

Vick's mouth moved again. From deep in the Wood, they heard Trix reply, "It's coming from over here. Quick! This way!"

There was a rustle in the leaves close behind them—too close— followed by a breathy, evil chuckle. A horde of tiny feet scampered into the Wood, following the voices.

Trix sat, open-mouthed, over the tiny flame that flickered up out of the flint and the leaves. Vick joined him, the shadows turning his face gaunt.

"Two can play at that game," said the leprechaun. "You two get some rest. We'll be off at first light."

8

The Blood Court

aving heard one too many tales of devious leprechauns, Trix woke every few minutes to keep an eye on Vick. He made sure that Trebald was safely hidden in Lizinia's hair before using his meager pack as a makeshift pillow. He hooked his arm through his bow, and placed his foot strategically beside Lizinia's The little man would back out of his offer to help them sneak into Faerie at the first opportunity; Trix didn't expect to see him come sunrise. But he didn't want to risk losing their weapons and what few supplies they had left to a light-finger in the process.

And yet, dawn came and Vick remained. The leprechaun not only graced them with his presence, but he'd also collected two pockets full of nuts, persimmons and crab apples. Trix was so famished that he'd forgotten he'd sworn off apples forever and gushed over the bounty. He reached for a crab apple, only to have it snatched from his fingers by a deceptively stealthy Trebald. "I saw it first, you rat!" cried Trix.

"That doesn't look like any rat I've ever seen," said Vick.

Trebald stuck his nose in the air and gave a definitive sniff in Vick's direction, whiskers twitching all the while. "Charlatan," he said to Trix. "Yes, yes."

"Be nice," warned Trix.

Trebald sank his pointed teeth into the meat of the apple and scurried back up Lizinia's arm to his hiding place.

"My pet," lied Lizinia. "You'll have to excuse him. He's shy." The sound of contented munching began to emanate from the back of her neck.

Vick, however, was more interested in Trix. "It spoke to you, didn't it?"

Trix didn't see any way to dodge the answer. "He said he was pleased to meet you."

"Oh, I highly doubt that." Vick waggled his finger at Trix. "You can talk to the animals. I've heard about you."

Trix shrugged. "It's not as impressive as it sounds." It would have been far more impressive had his ability been able to save them from the spriggans last night. Or the bumble bugs. Or the fetch. Trix considered their adventures of the evening before and weighed them against Vick's observation. Had the leprechaun been testing him?

Trix shook his head and reached for a persimmon. Exhaustion and hunger and the Faerie Queen's incessant compulsion were driving him positively mad. As if to illustrate the point, Trix looked up to see Papa Gatto perched on a branch of the tree, swinging his tail lazily and grinning deviously down upon them.

"What is he up to?" Trix said to Lizinia as she leaned in to retrieve a chestnut from the fire.

"Mischief," Lizinia said without looking up into the trees. She clearly did not feel it was wise to draw undue attention to her ethereal feline godfather.

Vick froze and his eyes widened. He turned to search the Wood behind him, but not before Papa Gatto had allowed the rays of the morning sun to erase him. When he turned back, he eyed Trix and Lizinia warily. "Please don't tell me there's some other bugaboo after us. I am not awake enough to deal with more nonsense."

Trix thought that a strange thing to say. The leprechaun had been awake enough to stoke the fire and forage for food, the latter of which must have taken a great deal of time.

"He means my brownie," said Lizinia. "He can be a bit of a troublemaker at times."

From beneath Lizinia's hair came a disgruntled snort, followed by more crabapple crunching. "Takes one to know one," Trebald mumbled with his mouth full.

Trix caught himself before the laugh escaped him, but Vick noticed. "He said something there too, didn't he?"

Trix stuffed his mouth with the rest of the persimmons.

Vick raised an eyebrow. As both the leprechaun's silver brows were as thick and bushy as his hair, it made an impressive gesture. "Don't be so humble, boy. Where we're about to go, only wild things reign. That little talent might actually save our hides."

Trix swallowed. "I'll do my best."

"You won't have a choice." Vick sighed, and then kicked dirt over the embers of the fire. "Ready then? Let's get this over with."

The deep of the Wood was only slightly less menacing in the daylight. After the strange encounters of the past evening, Trix concentrated on every creak of every branch and every rustle of every leaf, straining his already overtaxed mind. Even Lizinia jumped at shadows.

Trix scrutinized each animal that crossed their path. The free-roaming, unenchanted beasts in this part of the world intrigued Trix. Every other creature that snuck past them was a new discovery. There had been a family of large-eyed opossums with long fingers, a flock of tiny birds so rich in color that they looked like jewels dropping down from the sky, and a horned beetle with an elaborate indigo carapace.

"Steer clear there," Vick said of the last one. "The pads of its feet leave a venom that will give you nightmares for days. Not to mention a terrible itch." The leprechaun shuddered. "Learned that the hard way."

"Is it just me," Lizinia said softly, "or does it seem like everything in this forest is out to harm us?"

Vick moved a vine aside so that they could pass beneath it. "It's just nature responding to nature," he said. "Magic is thick in the air here, which means more ways to get captured and more traps to die in. The animals here have adapted in order to survive."

When they'd met him, Vick wanted nothing more than to be as far away from Faerie as his legs could carry him. Now he was leading them there, feeding them, and teaching them valuable lessons along the way? Trix bit his tongue and kept his suspicions to himself, but he remained wary of the spry little man.

"Goodness," said Lizinia. "Without fey magic to hinder them, those animals are possibly the most dangerous beasts in the Wood."

"That's about the size of it," said Vick. He came to a halt so quickly that Trix almost tripped over him. "The Hill is just beyond that grove. I need to get my bearings to find the entrance." He pointed to a fallen log. "You two rest there. And stay sharp."

Dutifully, Lizinia sat. "I thought I would be more relieved to be here," she said. "But now that we're almost to the Hill, I sort of wish we weren't."

"I know how you feel," Trix said as he joined her.

"Saturday said she would meet us here. Do you think we should stay and look for her a while before heading down into the Hill?"

Trix had been asking himself the same question all morning. He did want to wait for his sister. But he didn't want to waste any more time getting to the Faerie Queen. Nor did he want to give Vick time to change his mind. The leprechaun had decided to be helpful today, for whatever reason, and Trix fully intended to take advantage of that.

"Even if she finds a way to subdue Wolf while he's in animal form, we have no idea how long that will take," said Trix.

"And Wolf will stay an animal until we help the queen," said Lizinia. "Dilemma."

Trebald stuck his nose out from Lizinia's hair. "I can stay here and wait for her, yes?" asked the brownie. "I'm not in a hurry to rush down there. No, no."

"I'd have thought you'd be excited," said Trix. "Brownies love caves."

"Brownies love dark and quiet caves," said Trebald. "Not caves full of lions and tigers and bears and gods know what else. No, no."

"He's worried he might be prey for the larger beasts, is that it?" guessed Lizinia.

"Pretty much," said Trix.

Trebald nuzzled the clever girl's cheek in appreciation. His pointed teeth flashed in the sunlight.

Trix snapped his fingers. "We'll leave a mark on a tree." He pulled the golden dagger from his belt. "That way, Saturday will know we were here."

"Good idea," said Lizinia.

Trix carved a deep "T" into the trunk of the nearest silver birch. There had been a grove of silver birch near the towerhouse—when she was small, their youngest sister had declared the trees magic and refused to let Papa chop any of them down. Saturday might overlook a mark on other trees, but she would notice this one.

Vick emerged from the brush just as Trix was finishing. "If you're done carving your love notes, I've found the entrance. Follow me."

"He's charming," said Trebald. "Yes, yes. I'm so glad you picked him up."

"Someone's snarky when they're well rested," Trix said to the brownie.

The leprechaun assumed Trix was addressing him instead. "I do pride myself on my beauty sleep." With that, he pressed a knot on the tree and disappeared into a hole in the thick trunk.

Lizinia leaned into the tree and peered down into the black abyss. "It's terribly dark," she said.

Trix remembered back to the spriggans and held up his necklace with the tooth. "Dear Tooth," he said. "Does this entrance lead under the Hill?"

Wisdom's tooth sprang to light in affirmation.

"All right then," said Lizinia. "Lead the way, Wise Guy."

"I like her so much more than the nasty little man," said Trebald. "Yes, yes."

"Me too," Trix said to the brownie. He carved another quick "T" into this tree and led the way down.

The tree was so hollow, Trix wondered how it managed to stay alive at all. Carved into its wood was a steep staircase leading underground. The oaken steps turned to dirt, and then stone, twisting and turning, always down and down. Trix's ears popped. Thankfully, the light from Wisdom's tooth never waned.

Roots popped out of the walls at various intervals; Trix used them as rough handholds as they descended. The air was damp and cool and smelled like earth. Trix heard someone behind him take a deep breath. "Life and loam," sighed Trebald. "Yes, yes. I do miss this."

Eventually, the walls turned to rock, shot through with veins of black and gold that sparkled in the magical light. Lizinia's foot slipped on the step behind him and she caught Trix's shoulder to keep her balance.

"Are you all right?" he asked. "I can go slower, if you like."

"I'm fine," she said. "Just caught a bit of moss. How far down does he intend to take us?"

"To the center of the earth," Trix joked.

"Feels like it."

"Hey, Vick," Trix called out into the darkness. "Are we there yet?"

He would not have been surprised if the leprechaun had taken this opportunity to ditch them in the darkness, but a voice called back, "We are."

Trix lifted the tooth high in the air. Two steps below was a solid floor, and beyond that a large opening in the wall that led to an enormous ballroom. Tentatively, Trix and Lizinia stepped inside.

The ornate ceiling was so high that it almost disappeared into the darkness beyond the tooth's light. It was arched throughout, supported by a myriad of ornate pillars scattered about the room like festooned dancers. Each was more unique and elaborate than the ladies' dresses at the palace in Arilland.

"How is this entrance any kind of secret?" asked Lizinia.

Trix turned around. Behind them was no longer a stair but a gilded mirror at least twenty feet high.

"A magic mirror!" Trix was giddy at the thought. His sister Monday had a magic mirror, though he'd never seen it work. Trix was excited to finally have experienced a magic mirror firsthand, even if its only purpose was to hide the secret entrance to the Hill.

Now that he stood in front of a mirror, he could not help but notice his appearance. A young man stared back at him with wide, boyish eyes. Trix still wasn't used to that face. Being covered in filth from messy hair to dirty boots felt far more familiar. He didn't mind a bit, but it did look incredibly out of place in a majestic room like this. Lizinia wouldn't, though…where was Lizinia?

Trix looked for his companion in the mirror, but she wasn't there. He spun a slow circle with the tooth-light and found her crouched further down the wall.

"Trix, this woman needs help."

He raced to Lizinia's side. A woman sat on the floor like a rag doll, as if she'd slid down the wall from exhaustion and fallen asleep there. She wore a gossamer lilac ballgown...or what had at one point been a ballgown. It was in tatters now, torn to shreds and dotted with rust-colored streaks. Her long, dark hair was dotted with wilted wildflowers. Her arms and legs and neck and face were covered in bite marks.

"Not good," Trebald said from his perch on Lizinia's shoulder. "No, no."

Vick appeared out of the darkness. He knelt on the other side of the woman and lifted her wrist. When he released it, it fell limply to the floor. "This woman is beyond anyone's help."

"Those aren't animal bites," said Trix. "They're human. Many humans, by the look of it."

Lizinia raised a golden hand to her mouth. "Who would do such a thing?"

"The Blood Court," said Vick. Trix nodded, but Lizinia looked at him blankly, so the leprechaun went on. "There is a host of humans—mostly royalty—who live off the Faerie Court. They leave their kingdoms and castles and families behind so that they can stay here, under the Hill, forever."

"What's forever?" asked Lizinia. It was a fair question. She'd lived an enchanted life while the cats were alive, and they'd prolonged it further by trapping her in that house until Trix had come along and released her.

"Fairies and people with fey blood outlive humans," explained Trix. "Twice, sometimes five times as long. It's in their blood."

Vick held up the dead woman's bite-riddled arm. "Certain

fairies are willing to trade their blood for gold and trinkets, and certain humans will pay whatever it takes for immortality."

Papa had only told Trix one story of the Blood Court that he could remember. Velius, the Duke of Cauchemar, was cousin and advisor to King Rumbold of Arilland, and one of Saturday's sword fighting trainers. He was also riddled with fey magic, none of which he'd inherited from his human father. The older Veluis's father grew, the more jealous he became of his son that never seemed to age. Papa's story said that, on his death bed, Velius's father had disappeared under the Hill to join other humans like him, willing to drink fairy blood so that they might live a life far longer than nature intended.

Until he'd met Peregrine, Velius was the longest living person Trix had ever known. "And what is gold compared to everlasting life?"

"I'm certainly not the person to ask," said Lizinia. "But if fey magic is bound, is fairy blood still…effective?"

"No," said Vick.

"Wait," said Trix. "So, somewhere down here there's an army of bloodthirsty human royals?"

"I'd rather not wait, if it's all the same," said Vick. "I'd like to get out of here before they find us."

"I agree," said Lizinia.

"After you," Trix said to the leprechaun. As soon as he'd spoken the words, Wisdom's tooth brightened. It burned like a star, blinding them with its brilliance.

"Can't you douse that thing?" asked Vick.

Even if he knew of a way, he wasn't sure it would be particularly wise to stop anything the tooth advised. As Trix stepped away from his companions, the light caught the mirror they had passed through and reflected it back tenfold, illuminating the space from floor to ceiling. Trix now had a much clearer picture of the ballroom...and its occupants.

They were all well dressed, like the dead woman at their feet. Their suits and gowns were also torn and covered in the same rusty streaks that Trix knew now could only be blood. Their limbs were pale, their faces gaunt, and they moved listlessly, as if they had little energy left. Until they saw the party of hale, healthy young people, and then their vigor seemed to renew.

A hum began to fill the air around them. "Mmmmmmm...."

"Wasps?" whispered Trix.

"No, no," Trebald mumbled from the safety of Lizinia's hair.

The Blood Court moved in closer. Their eyes burned like red rubies in hollow sockets. A few of them had begun to drool.

"That is the sound hungry people make the moment that dessert is served." Vick began moving his hand along the wall, presumably looking for another exit, and muttering all the while. "Need to get out of here. We've stayed too long already. Gods, why did I come back underground..."

The leprechaun was concentrating so hard on finding a way out that he didn't notice when he bumped right into one of the Blood Court. Luckily, Vick was quicker and stronger than the woman, and he slipped out of her grasp. But there were more behind her. The ways out of this room were becoming increasingly blocked.

Trix pulled an arrow out of its quiver and had a thought. "Do you think you can do what you did to the spriggan?" he asked Lizinia.

The golden girl had already drawn her bow, but the golden star on her brow was furrowed. "Those were ghosts, Trix. I don't know if I can shoot a human. Even if we knew the same thing would happen that happened in the forest. Which we don't."

"Mmmmmmmmm...."

The humming grew louder. Vick pulled the hammer from his belt and lifted it high. They were surrounded now—fighting their way out seemed to be the only choice. Trix selected a member of the court, a tall man with several stars of office, aimed for one of his broad shoulders...and then the music started.

At the far end of the room, Trix made out a lithe shadow bent over what must have been a music box, for that's what the music sounded like, airy and tin. Amplified as it was by the shape of the ballroom, the song remained simple and understated. But it was enough.

The humming stopped. Compelled by the music, the members of the Blood Court broke into pairs and began to dance. They spun about the room with wild abandon, lost in the elementary strains. But for the smell of unwashed souls, dried blood, and impending death, it might have been beautiful.

The lithe shadow spun through the ragged dancers, weaving in and out among them, unnoticed by those lost in the melody. But not unrecognized by Trix.

"Wednesday!" he cried, for it was indeed his third-oldest sister. Wednesday, with her raven hair and deep indigo eyes, had left for Faerie only a few months ago to be apprenticed to their Aunt Joy. Wednesday had more magic in her than anyone Trix knew. Except Aunt Joy and her twin Sorrow. And maybe Velius. And possibly Mama.

"Come quickly," whispered his shadow sister. "They will stop when the music stops."

"Did you cast a spell?" asked Trix. If anyone could summon magic when there was none to be had, it would be Wednesday.

"Muscle memory," she said, waving them down a dark corridor. "Eating, sleeping, and dancing are all these people have ever done. And for some, even sleep is optional."

Wisdom's light waned as they sped down hallways and through doorways that reminded Trix of the Palace in Arilland, if the palace had been built in the bowels of the earth. The tooth extinguished itself altogether as Wednesday reached for an ornate door handle. For the first time in many days, Trix's soul felt at peace. They had come to the end of their journey.

"Thank you," he said to the tooth as he replaced it beneath his shirt.

Wednesday pulled open the door.

The snarling bear behind it had been waiting for them.

9

The Bear Prince and the Magic Sister

he bear went straight for Vick. It leapt upon him, both beast and leprechaun tumbling into the hall in a blur of snowy fur and hair. Lizinia stepped in and used her considerable strength to push the bear back into the room. The bear snapped; the leprechaun shrieked. Vick raised his hammer for the attack.

"Don't hurt him!" Wednesday cried.

Trix grabbed at the hammer until he wrenched it out of Vick's hand.

"You fool! He's going to kill me!"

The bear shoved Lizinia aside and came at the leprechaun again, knocking Vick backward onto the floor. The beast pinned the leprechaun's arms down with his enormous clawed feet, trapping the rest of the small man's body with his own.

"I told you these rabid beasts were out of their minds!" cried

Vick. "Get him off of me before he swallows me whole!"

The bear stuck his nose into Vick's face and growled, low and unceasingly. If the bear truly had intended to kill Vick, the little man would be dead already.

Trix put his hands on his hips and assessed the situation. "I don't know, Vick. I'm familiar with bears and I have to say…this seems personal."

Brave Wednesday walked around to face the bear. She reached out a slender finger and stroked the animal between the eyes until it stopped growling and looked up at her.

"Uncle Bear, that's enough," she said.

The bear snorted at her like a petulant horse. Less impressively, Wednesday snorted back.

"What are you doing?" yelled Vick. "Don't goad him! He's going to eat me!"

Wednesday pointed to Vick with her free hand. "Hush!" The bear was easing into her petting now. She gently persuaded the bear off of Vick, who let out an exaggerated grunt once the weight left him. Lizinia went to help him up.

"Trix," Wednesday said as she directed the great animal to the other side of the room, "I would like you to meet our uncle, the Bear Prince."

"Family," Vick said as he stood up and brushed himself off. "Of course. Madness thrives in the blood."

"Hello, Uncle Bear," Trix said cheerfully. "I'm Trix Woodcutter. These are my companions, Lizinia and Trebald."

Uncle Bear snorted, but said nothing.

"Did he say anything to you?" asked Lizinia.

"No words that I could make out so far," said Trix. He didn't think it too terribly odd. They had just arrived, after all, and it was possible his uncle was still processing everything. On top of that, some animals were just naturally reticent.

Trix and Lizinia both greeted Uncle Bear with a pat. Trebald scurried down Lizinia's arm to nuzzle his whiskers in the bear's soft fur—quite the recommendation from the timid brownie. "Good man," said Trebald. "Yes, yes." Then he hopped from his perch to the floor and fled into the dark corners of the room.

"I want to try something, if that's all right?" he asked his sister. Wednesday, who could still read his mind without magic, nodded.

Trix took a deep breath in, and then slowly exhaled. He hadn't been able to get this chance with Wolf—if he managed to communicate with his uncle, then perhaps they could get to the bottom of this spell. Perhaps they hadn't lost Wolf forever.

Trix knelt before the bear, making himself as small as he could and putting his entire body in the animal's line of sight. He called upon the knack he used to speak to animals every day, as well as the annoyingly dormant animal magic inside him. "I am Trix," he said, slowly. "Your nephew. Can you understand me?"

Normally, when animals responded to Trix, their voices came to him as clearly as if he were speaking to another person. Uncle Bear's voice seemed...trapped. Trix read the subtle shift in his expression—the bear had understood him, but seemed unable to respond.

Trix stared deeper into his uncle's black eyes and tried again. This time, flashes appeared before him: scenes from another life. Roses. Fire. A young woman's smile. A whip. Blood. Gold. Trees.

The images shot through him like a rain of arrows, but he could make no sense of them. With his next breath, he could hear the fire. He could smell the Wood. He felt something wrap around his body like a second skin, surrounding him, comforting him...and then suffocating him.

Uncle Bear growled and bucked away, breaking the contact. Trix gasped for air. Bear moved his jaws to make words, but they all came out in moan-speak and nonsensical barks. Trix moved his arm quickly out of the way of his uncle's excellent teeth.

"I can't..." Trix shook his head. He wasn't even sure how to explain what had just happened. "I can't hear him," he said finally, for lack of better words.

"So much for that gods-given talent," said Vick. "Let's go find you the Faerie Queen already."

The bear snapped in Vick's direction, but made no move to attack the leprechaun further. Regardless, it was enough to send Vick cowering into the corner, well out of claws' reach.

Trix tried to soothe his uncle with calm words. "I don't know if you can hear what I'm saying, but I think I understand your frustration."

Wednesday moved to stand beside them. She reached out and scratched their uncle gently behind one ear. "He's been fey for so long."

"His body took fey form because he fell in love with Aunt Snow, didn't it?" asked Trix.

"Love is a powerful thing," Wednesday cooed, more to the bear than to her brother.

"I'm sure his bear-self is just out of practice," said Trix. "After we've spent more time together we'll be able to communicate better."

"Jolly," Trix heard Vick murmur from behind a curtain. His opinion was followed by an "Ow!" that sounded very much like someone being bitten by a brownie. Trix made a mental note to thank Trebald later.

"No, no. Don't hurt the bear." Trix turned to see Aunt Joy emerge from a room in the back where, presumably, she had been lying down. Her clothes were a rumpled mess. The black hair that was typically tied up in a neat coif sagged limply about her shoulders and the cameo at her throat hung from a ripped collar. Aunt Joy was a less gaunt, slightly older version of Wednesday…but the last time Trix had seen her she looked considerably more put together.

"Our Bear." Aunt Joy turned in circles across the room before wrapping her arms around the bear's large head. "Little Bear. Pretty Bear." She repeated the words over and over until they became a song.

"*Little* Bear?" Trix said wryly. "Wednesday, what's going on?"

"She's been like this since the magic was bound. Snow White fell into a sleep we could not wake her from, and Uncle Bear went mad."

Where Aunt Joy's indigo eyes were dreamily unfocused, Wednesday's eyes were clear. Trix found this highly unusual in itself—Wednesday was the sister who wandered away with her sentences half-finished, reciting poetry that may or may not have ever been written, and speaking in languages from no country on any known map. On her best days, Wednesday was typically as coherent as a cat.

"She's been like this," said Trix, "but what happened to *you?*"

Wednesday cast her eyes to the floor, but Trix could make out a half-smile on her lips. "Aunt Joy is pure fey," she answered. "You and I are tainted with other blood."

With the fey magic bound, Trix had assumed the human in his blood was what kept him from becoming as muddled as Bear. But what other blood did Wednesday have? God blood? Demon blood? Trix would have believed either. Or both. How many types of magic were there in the world? "So…the fey magic was making you mad this whole time?"

"Many magics call my head a home," she said cryptically, sounding much more like the Wednesday he knew. "They're constantly fighting, screaming… I lose myself in their war." She closed her eyes; put a hand to her temple. "Without the fey magic, my soul's voice is louder, and I can fight. For the first time, I can fight back."

Before this journey, Trix couldn't have imagined the powers at work in Wednesday's mind. But all the voices, the visions, the strange compulsions, the crawling skin, the sense that his magic was broken even though he knew for a fact that an outside force was to blame… Yes, now he had a pretty good idea of what it was like to be Wednesday Woodcutter. And as soon as they freed the fey magic, she would be trapped again in her own mind. The thought broke his heart.

But there was no time to waste. The Blood Court could find them at any moment, and who knew what other animals, crazed with wild magic, might come clawing at their door.

"Did Aunt Snow fall asleep first, or was the magic bound first?" Trix asked Wednesday. "Can you remember?"

"It was Aunt Snow. Her condition put Uncle Bear in a furious state long before he even changed into a bear. And then when he did I couldn't change him back by myself, so I looked for Aunt Joy and found her…like that." Joy was still petting the bear as if he were a tiny puppy. The bear didn't seem to mind. "I've kept them separated for fear that they might hurt each other without meaning to."

"I'll put her back to bed," offered Lizinia. She approached Joy and the bear slowly, so as not to startle them. Once Aunt Joy caught sight of the golden girl, she was enraptured.

"All of this mess…there's only one answer that makes sense," Trix said to Wednesday.

Wednesday nodded. "Aunt Sorrow."

"Sorrow. Sister. Sadness." Joy's words turned into a little tune as Lizinia herded her back to her room.

"Sister Sorrow, Sister Sadness,

No tomorrow ends the madness.

Greatest of seven, first at the gate,

Oldest by birth and cursedest by fate."

"'Cursedest?'" asked Trix.

Wednesday shrugged. The gesture was so very unlike Wednesday that Trix had to suppress a snort of laughter.

There were seven Mouton sisters: Sorrow, Joy, Teresa, Tesera, Snow White, Rose Red, and Mama. Sorrow was Joy's twin—just as powerful and twice as mischievous. Aunt Joy had spent most of her life cleaning up Sorrow's messes.

Of all the Woodcutter siblings, Sorrow had caused Wednesday the most pain. To balance the scales, Wednesday had helped Joy magically imprison the soul of Sorrow's lover, the evil King Hargath, before he and Sorrow could do even more damage.

"Sorrow is stealing her sisters' powers," Trix said "She has all of them but Rose Red now. And Joy."

Wednesday gasped. "That means…"

"She has Mama's power. Now everything Sorrow says will come true."

"That's how she bound the fey magic," said Wednesday. "It has to be. I'm not sure even the gods have that much power. And even if they did…"

"But where did she bind the magic?" asked Trix. "How are we supposed to look for it with the Blood Court and who knows how many wild animals roaming the halls? And how will we know when we find it?"

"You'll know," Wednesday said with complete confidence.

"Fantastic," said the leprechaun behind the curtain.

Lizinia exited Joy's bedroom and closed the door quietly. "She sang herself to sleep. What did I miss?"

"My terrible aunt has stolen even more terrible powers, and she's trapped the fey magic somewhere we'll never find it." Trix clung to hope as despair swept over him. What would Aunt Joy say at a time like this? *Family is forever*, his wise aunt would say. *Family will break the world and family will fix it, on and on until the end of time.*

"Fate wouldn't have wanted the world torn apart by magic," said Lizinia. "I wager it's still here somewhere, under the Hill. We just have to find it."

Wednesday grinned at the golden girl's optimism. "She reminds me of Sunday."

"Trix often compares me to his sisters, and I always take it as a compliment," Lizinia said with a smile. "Besides, Vick will help us out."

"I will do no such thing," said the curtain. There was a rustle followed by the stomping of feet, and Vick came tearing back into the room with Trebald hot on his heels. "Bite me again, rat, and I'll have you for dinner!"

"No!" cried Wednesday. "No eating anything while you're here!"

Trebald stopped dead in his tracks. "*What?*"

"I'm sorry," said Wednesday. "With everything going on I didn't think to mention it until now."

Trix's hand drifted to his stomach. Those persimmons suddenly felt very small and very long ago. Trix had rushed them along so fast that he hadn't even considered replenishing their packs. He thanked the gods for Vick's generosity that morning, whatever the leprechaun's true motives.

"Anything?" Lizinia motioned to a bowl on a side table. "Those berries look fine from here."

"You're welcome to try them," said Vick.

"Fairy fare is poisonous to humans and animals," said Wednesday. "Fey magic is the only thing that makes it palatable. Before this Faerie Queen's reign, anyone who ate the food under the Hill was bound to remain here forever."

Trebald spat. "I bit the little man earlier, yes, yes. Does that count?" The brownie began to tremble, which meant he was nervous, which meant he'd be hungry. Lizinia scooped up the brownie and tried to console him as well as she could.

Vick didn't need translation. "Do I look like fairy food to you, rat?"

"Enough, you two," said Lizinia. "We have some magic to find, and Vick's going to help us find it."

The leprechaun crossed his arms. "We might as well be looking for a needle in a haystack."

Trix had been forced to do that once, after he'd "lost" his sister Friday's needle so that she'd stop mending laundry and play with him. The fact that the needle was magic had not made the finding of it any easier.

"Look for an object that stands out," Wednesday clarified. "Something special, like your dagger"—she pointed to Trix— "or…you," she pointed to Lizinia. "The obvious thing would be a vessel of some sort."

This Wednesday was so serious and straight to the point, it kept throwing Trix off guard. Wednesday-before would have long since fluttered off to chase butterflies in the dark. "How do you know all this?"

Vick narrowed his eyes at Wednesday. "Are you sure you don't know where the fey magic is?"

"I wish I did," said Wednesday. "I only know it has to be a vessel because that's how Aunt Joy and I bound the essence of King Hargath. It was part of my training."

"What vessel did you use for that spell?" asked Lizinia.

"A crystal ball on one of the Faerie Queen's scepters."

"I would start there, yes?" said Trebald. "With the rest of her scepters. Yes, yes."

Trix's patience was wearing thin. "How about we start by *finding the Faerie Queen?*"

The leprechaun still looked dubious. "We still have to trek through an entire Hill full of vast caverns and untold dangers. You may be able to charm the animals, wonderboy, but you don't know what horrible fate awaits you out there. You thought the Wood was bad? Ha! You have no idea!"

"That's why we have you," said Lizinia.

Trix stared down at the leprechaun. "If you were going to steal a magical item from the Faerie Queen, where would you go first?"

"The catacombs," the leprechaun said all too quickly, and then pursed his lips.

Trix straightened, proud of himself for finally catching Vick in the act of withholding information. "The catacombs it is, then."

"But what if the Blood Court finds us again?" asked Lizinia.

"The Blood Court!" Wednesday cried out. "That's how you can search for the magic without being noticed. We'll dress you like the Blood Court!"

Trix wasn't sure who Wednesday meant by "we," but the idea was crazy enough to have come from Wednesday-before, so Trix was intrigued.

"Trix, you and the leprechaun——"

"I have a name," said Vick.

"——can borrow something of Uncle Bear's. It will all be too big for you of course, but..." Wednesday's voice trailed off. She looked Trix over from head to toe, as if seeing him for the first time. "You've grown."

Trix straightened his shoulders. The last time he'd seen Wednesday, he'd been a scrawny slip of a fey boy. Now he was a young man with a cat's curse. "You noticed."

Wednesday tapped her chin. "Mmm. It suits you. Now, your friend here is more of a challenge."

"Lizinia," said Lizinia.

"Lizinia," Wednesday repeated. "I won't remember that. I'm sorry."

"It's all right," said Lizinia. "I forgive you in advance."

"That means more to me that you will ever know," said Wednesday. "Lizinia, what do you have in your packs?"

"Not much," she said.

"Definitely not clothes," said Trix.

"Let me see," said Wednesday.

Obligingly, Trix dumped his pack onto the table. They had flint, a bit of twine, a bunch of clean rags, a sewing kit, fish hooks, and the green fairy stone Saturday had given him. Lizinia pulled the matching pink stone out of her pocket and added it to the collection.

"A-ha!" Wednesday ran her finger over the fairy stones. She picked up the pink one and turned to Lizinia. "Give me your hand."

Trebald scurried up Lizinia's arm, freeing her hand up so that she could slip it into Wednesday's. Wednesday turned her face to the heavens with her eyes closed, a stance with which Trix was all to familiar.

"There's no fey magic," Trix reminded her. "Why bother attempting a spell? You've already said you failed before."

Wednesday cracked one eye open and peeked down at her brother. "I let you try something with Bear. Now hush. It's my turn."

"Yes, Mama," Trix teased.

Wednesday ignored him and closed her eyes again. "Lizinia,

who turned you into gold?"

"The cats," said Lizinia. Her eyes were not closed. "One cat in particular, named Papa Gatto. He was a godfather of sorts."

"Still is," muttered Trix.

"I said hush," scolded Wednesday. "Cat magic? Hmm." Her smile turned mischievous. "Might be just strange enough to work."

"But I don't have any magic," said Lizinia. "I'm not a cat. I'm just—"

"—a vessel," finished Wednesday. "Through you, I can theoretically amplify whatever non-fey magic is buried inside me."

"Theoretically?" asked Vick.

"Since your fairy stone was magical to begin with, I should only need a very little to change it into...aha!" In the blink of an eye, the fairy stone had transformed into a ballgown. An enormous, full-skirted, gossamer and silk, glimmering *pink* ballgown spilled out of Wednesday's free hand.

Lizinia gasped. "Is that for *me*?" she said dreamily.

"That's the idea," said Wednesday.

"But I can't take off my clothes," said Lizinia.

"We'll just slip it right over what you have on," said Wednesday. "The gold will complement it nicely. Now, come on. I'll help you in here while the men get dressed."

"Help me?" Lizinia tilted her head. "It's been a long time since I've needed to change clothes, but I do remember that I never had anyone help me do anything."

"Not straighten your dress or comb your hair? Nothing?" Wednesday was flabbergasted. "Didn't you have a mother? Or sisters?"

"One of each," said the golden girl. "But I never had kindness to go with them."

Wednesday gave Lizinia a hug. "Well, you do today. Come on."

Trix loved his mad sister all over again, and not just for the ridiculous amount of magic she shouldn't have been able to do. He dragged Vick into Uncle Bear's bedchamber—the room was decorated in rich reds and golds, with a four-poster bed almost large enough to accommodate his uncle's pure beast form.

"It feels strange rummaging through someone else's clothes," said Trix. "Even if he is my uncle."

Vick had no such compunction. Within moments the leprechaun had opened all the drawers and tossed most of the contents on the ground. Trix collected a clean shirt and trousers. Trix had grown, but Uncle Bear's shirt was still too big for him; the sleeves covered most of his hands and the hem fell to mid-thigh. Vick helped him shorten the sleeves with the golden dagger, and then Trix used the dagger to cut Vick a tunic from one of Uncle Bear's fancy pillow cases.

Trix pinned on a few medals and examined himself in the looking glass. The boots he wore were only slightly scuffed, his chin had only the faintest shadow of stubble, and his eyes were far too clear. He looked less like a member of the Blood Court and more like an imposter trying to pass as a member of the Blood Court. "At least I'm still covered in dirt and ash and slime and sweat and who knows what else."

"All the better for your disguise," said Vick. "It's not like the Blood Court is frequenting the baths themselves."

A bath. Considering all the times he'd almost drowned recently he never thought he'd miss bathing again, but a bath suddenly seemed like the most decadent thing in the world. A bath and Mama's potato-leek stew. His mouth began to water. He needed a distraction before he gulped down those tempting berries in the foyer.

"I'd like to take Uncle Bear with us," Trix said to Vick.

"No way," said the leprechaun. "You can have me, or that infernal beast, but not both."

"He hasn't harmed you, and he won't. Lizinia and I will make sure of that."

"Forgive me if I don't trust you," said Vick.

Trix didn't trust Vick either, but he didn't feel it wise to point that out. "My hope is that the closer we get to the fey magic, even if it's trapped, the better we'll be able to communicate. Which would solve two problems: helping us find the fey magic itself, and helping us figure out exactly what's going on."

Vick snorted. "Then you don't need me."

"My *hope* is that it will work. If all my hopes came true, none of this would have ever happened. Please, Vick. Please help me find the Faerie Queen." Trix tried to think of what else he could say to convince the leprechaun. "I will make sure that you're adequately compensated for your time and trouble."

"Fine," Vick said after a long pause. "But you better keep that overgrown snowball and that bite-happy rat away from me."

"I promise," said Trix. Just as they stepped back over the threshold in the entranceway, the opposite door opened and Lizinia emerged.

Wednesday had worked wonders. Lizinia's golden hair was

pinned up into a formal coif with strands of red ribbon and rose petals. The creamy pink silk was gathered into loops that draped down her arms from her golden shoulders and across her bodice. Enormous layers of skirt fell to the floor in a blush waterfall covering her functional golden work skirt completely. She caught Trix's appreciative eye and smiled, which seemed to make her whole body glow. She was *perfect*.

It would never do.

Trix crossed the room in a few short strides, scooping up a handful of berries from the side table in one hand, and scooping up Lizinia with the other. While she was still confused about his intentions, he kissed her...and smashed his handful of berries into the bodice of her pristine pink dress.

With a squeal, Lizinia twisted out of Trix's embrace and pulled his hair, but the voluminous skirt tripped her up and she pitched to the floor. Trix caught her before she hit the flagstones, pulling her back to her feet and tearing a sleeve of the dress in the process. The thin pink fabric split easily, revealing the gold beneath, and the small dark smudge where the spriggan had touched her.

"Trix Woodcutter! That's the first pretty dress I've had in a million years, and you had to go ruin it." Lizinia secured the last few berries in the bowl. "But two can play at this game." She returned fire with one hand and used the other to tear his sleeve.

"I'll protect you, little brother," Wednesday cried. She picked up a stray bit of ammunition on the floor and threw it...smack between Vick's eyes.

Berry juice dripped down the leprechaun's nose. "You'll pay for that, fey witch!"

For a few blissful moments, the room was filled with joyful screams and the tart fragrance of inedible fey berries. Trebald joined in as well, scurrying around their feet, trying to trip them, and sometimes succeeding. When the bowl was empty, Trix resisted the urge to lick his fingers, wiping the remnants on his shirt instead before he helped Lizinia up off the floor.

Their clothes were ripped and covered in red stains. His hair was even more mussed and matted, Lizinia's artfully arranged locks had been mostly undone. It was tough to say who was a worse disaster.

Wednesday clapped her hands together. "You look perfect!"

Trix bowed.

Lizinia fluffed her tattered gown. "I feel better about this disguise already."

Vick pulled at his tunic. "Speak for yourself."

Trix bent an arm for Lizinia to take. "Shall we, my dear?"

"We shall." The golden girl laid her hand on the inside of his elbow, as if she was a highborn lady who did such things every day of her life. "Let's go find some magic."

10

The Catacombs

rix, Lizinia, Vick, and Uncle Bear snuck into the corridor. The wan light of Wisdom's tooth lit the way. Vick, who should have been in the lead, exercised his right to cowardice by barking guidance from the back of the group.

They had been running on their way to Wednesday's chambers. They proceeded more cautiously when leaving, which gave Trix a chance to look around as Vick steered them through the maze of hallways. The walls and ceiling were fashioned from the Hill itself—the halls were lushly decorated with flowers and vines that seemed to grow from within. Here and there something scuffled in the darkness beyond the circle of toothlight, but no animal approached them.

"Was it wise to leave Trebald behind?" Lizinia whispered to Trix. "I'd gotten quite used to him."

Trix was more concerned about leaving their bows, but as Wednesday pointed out, long range weapons wouldn't be useful in such close quarters. Lizinia, Uncle Bear, and his golden dagger would have to be enough. "Trebald will be fine. He'll know Saturday when she arrives, and he'll be able to track us by scent and lead her to us when she does. Besides, this trip would make him terribly nervous, and you know he gets hungry when he's nervous."

"That's true. I will worry about him less this way. He is safe."

Trix wasn't sure anywhere under the Hill was safe while magic was out of balance, but there was a far better chance of it with Wednesday and Aunt Joy. Abruptly, the decorative hallway forked. The flowers that lined the right side were all yellow. The flowers on the left were all a vibrant fuchsia.

"Purple," Vick said from the vicinity of Uncle Bear's hindquarters.

Trix and Lizinia complied. "Are *you* hungry?" Lizinia asked him.

"I prefer not to think about it." Trix couldn't afford to be trapped in Faerie forever and ever. Wouldn't his wicked Aunt Sorrow have loved that?

"Left again," said Vick, but Trix and Lizinia halted instead. An enormous blue-and-green striped python stretched across the junction.

Lizinia, with her impervious skin, thought nothing of the blockade and moved to step over the snake's thick body. It was Uncle Bear who caught a golden arm in his jaws and pulled her back.

"I'm not worried about being bitten," Lizinia said to the bear before realizing he probably wouldn't understand a word. "Tell him I'm not worried," she said to Trix.

Vick popped out from behind Uncle Bear. "You might not be troubled by fangs, but you still need air to breathe, don't you?"

Lizinia took a step back from the large body. "Yes."

"A python's hugs can be quite unyielding," said Trix.

"I didn't intend to stop and introduce myself," said Lizinia.

Vick examined the milky scales and harrumphed. "Be wary at any rate. That's the Lady Shahmaran. Her hugs are deadly enough when she's in fey form. And if those don't kill you, her scent will."

The pearlescent scales caught the magic light of the tooth and shimmered mesmerizingly. Trix hoped this meant the python had chosen to move along peacefully. He peeked around the corner to make sure this was the case.

Lady Shahmaran stared back at him. The scales around those mythical eyes were much darker green, almost black. The ornate hood culminated in an orange-gold crown at the top of her viciously pointed head. Her tongue tasted the air before him, air that now smelled cloyingly of gardenias.

"Trix Woodcutter…milady," he said when he found his voice, though he couldn't seem to speak much above a whisper. "We're trying to find the Faerie Queen. Can you help us?"

Lady Shahmaran did not have eyebrows to raise in her animal form, but Trix could tell that "we" and "us" caught her attention. Her magnificent head slipped past him to peer at the rest of his party. She stared down Uncle Bear, and then Lizinia, and then Vick with equal measure. At last, she returned to Trix.

"*SNAKE*," said Lady Shahmaran, and then her substantial body slipped like water into the darkness.

"Did she speak to you?" Lizinia asked Trix.

"What did she say?" asked Vick.

"Nothing," answered Trix. "She seemed to be aware of what she was, of her animal self, but she did not say anything helpful beyond that."

Vick elbowed him in the hip. "Powers getting a little rusty, eh, Prophecy Boy?"

"Shame," said Lizinia.

Vick turned to the golden girl. "Yes. It's a shame that Lady Shahmaran went along her merry way without killing us. Tragic, I tell you. Shall we get on with this?"

The next hallway was brighter. Gem-studded wall sconces flowed seamlessly into the architecture, scattering multicolored light all around them. Trix was surprised that he hadn't yet tripped over anything covering the floor, an intricate design of roots, moss, and grass. Gradually, the softer surface shifted to polished stone. Bear's claws clicked along in the silence.

Flowering plants grew up from the earth and flourished along the side of the hall, though there seemed to be no water source or opportunity for sunlight. Upon closer inspection, Trix realized that the leaves of the foliage sagged with wilt. A riot of petals blanketed the floor. Fey magic had been sustaining these plants. Without it, they would soon die.

"Don't go," chirped the birds perched among the flowers.

"Turn back," they said. "Don't go. Not here."

"Can you hear them?" Lizinia asked Trix.

"Can't you?" Vick asked sharply. The leprechaun covered his ears. "Chatterboxes. Give a body a headache with all that racket."

The staccato song saddened Trix's heart. "They're warning us away." And yet, he still felt the pull of the Faerie Queen, stronger than ever, urging him on.

"Wise birds," said Lizinia.

"Do you suppose we could eat *them?*" asked Vick.

Trix ignored the leprechaun. He had heard birds in the Wood call for food, or warning, or mating, but rarely sadness, and never in such numbers. Such a feeling could only come from animals who had once been men and women. "These are people," Trix told him.

"They *were* people," corrected Vick.

"And they will be again," Lizinia stated defiantly.

Trix wanted to hug the birdfolk, to take them up in his arms and rescue them from whatever they felt was so frightening. He wanted to give them that safety he could not promise. "We're on our way to fetch the Faerie Queen," he said reassuringly.

A red bird and a bluebird flew out of the brush and alighted upon Trix's shoulders.

"Trapped!" tweeted the red one.

"Trapped!" tweeted the blue.

Before long, the whole hallway rang out in a deafening chorus. "Traptraptraptraptraptraptrap!"

"Can't you shut them up?" Vick yelled at Trix.

"Too late!" cried Lizinia.

Beneath the birds' chatter, a low hum resonated from the other end of the hall. An involuntary shiver swept through Trix. Now that he wasn't sure when and where his next meal would come from, he recognized that sound. It was the sound of desperation. It was the sound of a hunger nothing could sate. It was the sound an empty stomach made when food was in sight.

"It's the Blood Court," he whispered. There were only two ways out of this stretch of hallway: the way forward, and the way back.

"How did they find us so fast?" asked Lizinia. "Did the birds tell them we were here?"

Trix opened his mouth to tell her exactly what the birds had said, but Vick answered her question before Trix had a chance to speak. "It's because we're going back to the ballroom."

"What?" asked Trix.

"Why?" asked Lizinia.

Bear's rumbling growl might have almost been a laugh.

The leprechaun threw up his hands. "Because the secret stair is the best way to the catacombs."

"You didn't think it wise to mention that before?" said Trix.

"I didn't think it mattered!" said Vick. "We have our costumes, and you were half prepared to run into them again anyway, weren't you?"

"We do," Lizinia said, far more judiciously than Trix would have. "And we are. But it would have been nice to know anyway."

Vick shrugged and tugged on his berry-stained tunic. "In my line of work, I've learned not to trust anyone."

Bear smiled at the leprechaun, displaying rows of dangerous teeth. It did not exactly come across as the kind gesture Trix hoped it was.

"Well," said Lizinia, "I guess it's time to see how well our disguises work."

Trix pulled his golden dagger from its sheath. "Judging by the sound of them, I don't think they'll be mistaking any of us for any of them." Trix faced Bear and concentrated with all his might. "We need to get through them, Uncle." He spoke slowly and evenly, to make sure his uncle had the greatest chance of understanding. Bear sniffed Trix's hair and licked his face, sending the birds on his shoulders back into the air. With a snarl, he arched his back and barreled past them to the dark end of the hall.

Lizinia followed with a battlecry that set Trix's blood and feet running after her. Vick raced to keep up.

Bear burst into the ballroom, knocking the Blood Court down like ninepins and clearing the path as he ran. The hindrance was only temporary, however—Trix turned back once to see the fallen men and women regain their footing and come after them again, hungry mouths agape and ruby red eyes shining from the shadows. More members of the Blood Court poured in from entrances all around the room—it seemed their number had doubled since that first encounter.

The four of them made it halfway to the mirror before they were surrounded. Vick held his hammer high.

"Don't hurt them if you can," Trix said to him. "It's not their fault that they've become these monsters."

"Don't be so naive, kid," said Vick. "This whole situation is entirely their fault. They paid handsomely for the privilege. And if it comes down to them or me"—he swung the hammer in a neat arc—"I choose them."

"I choose *me*," said Lizinia. She raised her bright arms above her head and spun herself away from the party. She might not have had a drop of blood anywhere inside her, but that enormous glittering dress and all the shiny gold certainly drew the eyes of the Blood

Court. Men and women came at her from all directions. They caught handfuls of her skirt and yanked until it shredded. A woman in a dark blue gown fell at Lizinia's feet and rolled beneath her gown to trip her.

It worked. Lizinia fell backward into a heap of pink skirt and two men jumped directly on top of her. The first one who attempted to take a bite of her howled in pain.

"Serves you right!" yelled Vick.

The one who hadn't sampled Lizinia's gold yet—a slender, black-haired man with a lace collar and vest full of decorative medals—turned to Vick and Trix. His eyes blazed even redder than before.

"I think he's figured it out," said Vick.

Bear moved to stand over Lizinia, shoving Court members out of the way and then threatening them with growls and sharp teeth if they dared try to approach again. Trix ran in to grab a golden hand and help her up. "Let's get to the mirror," he said. "Hurry!"

Vick planted his hammer squarely in the kneecap of the rotund man who had been waiting for Trix and the ballroom filled with more howls.

"You're welcome," said the leprechaun.

Bear used his body to knock people out of the way, but there were too many of them. Lizinia took up the rear, pulling lords and ladies off of Vick and Trix when they got too close. She even punched a few of them. Saturday would be so proud. Vick continued to aim for kneecaps, where he could find them, and Trix used the pommel of his dagger to make his own punches more effective. It would have been easy to cut the Blood Court with his dagger—too easy—but he couldn't bring himself to harm these poor, pitiful humans who'd been reduced to nothing but empty stomachs. Especially when he felt on the border of that very state himself.

Just as they reached the mirror, the black-haired man with the medals slipped through their defenses. He caught Trix's free arm and yanked it toward him. Lizinia grabbed the man by his dark hair and dragged him away, leaving deep scratches on the inside of Trix's elbow.

"The mirror!" yelled the leprechaun.

Trix blinked and ran for the glass. Bear stopped short of the mirror but Trix flung himself at it, determined to pass right through its surface as easily as they had when they'd used the secret entrance to enter the ballroom. But he did not pass through. With a thud, Trix's bottom hit the ground.

"Doesn't it work from this side?" asked Lizinia.

"It's magic," said Vick. "We have to ask its permission—"

"Dear mirror, will you please let us through?" Lizinia said hurriedly.

"—in rhyme," Vick finished.

Of course. Trix remembered that now. Monday's looking glass needed a rhyme to work. Saturday's might have, had she not smashed it before they could try it properly. Which was really too bad, since Saturday was great at rhymes. She and Peter always played word games while working in the Wood.

Trix did not share that ability. *Oh, Saturday, why aren't you here?* Even Lizinia's infernal spectral godfather would be more helpful than he felt at this moment.

Lizinia, ever the optimist, tried her best in vain. "Mirror, dearer, clearer... Oh, I am horrible at this. What about you, Vick?"

"I've never been fond of mirrors," said the leprechaun.

"I'm sure the feeling's mutual," said Trix. It was unkind of him, but the pain in his arm coupled with the emptiness in his stomach and head did not put him in a generous mood.

"At least let him try," Lizinia scolded him.

Vick, sufficiently annoyed, kicked the glass. "LET US THROUGH, YOU LOUSY PIECE OF—"

Lizinia put a hand on Vick's arm. "Now, Vick. You catch more flies with honey."

The leprechaun pointed at the swarm of courtiers. "*They* don't want honey. *They* want blood."

The biting and smacking and howling and growling and humming from the Blood Court made Trix gag. They didn't have time for this, but his mind was blank. Well, not blank. But, "*Save us, Trix Woodcutter. Save us all*" did not rhyme.

Out of nowhere, Lizinia began to sing.

"*Lavender's blue,*

Rosemary's green..."

Trix finished the verse.

"*Oh how I wish*

We could find the queen."

Lizinia smiled triumphantly and started the next lines, loud enough to mask the Blood Court's frenzy.

"*Rosemary's green,*

Lavender's blue..."

This time it was Vick who chimed in.

"I'm gonna regret

Ever meeting you."

"Come on, Vick," urged Lizinia. "You can do better."

Vick gritted his teeth, spun in a circle, and stopped with his feet planted in front of the mirror. He leaned back and yelled into it at the top of his lungs. "How do you do, oh looking glass? Now let us back through, you pain in the a—aaaaaagh!"

Uncle Bear, who had been watching the scene carefully, stuck his snout right in the middle of Vick's back and nudged him not-so-gently through the face of the mirror the second its reflective surface began to melt away. Then Bear picked up Trix by the scruff of his borrowed shirt and leapt through the magic glass himself. Lizinia was the last to join them...as was the female courtier who'd caught hold of her arm.

"Quick!" she called. "Close it off!"

Trix might not have known much about magic mirrors, but he was familiar enough with enchanted animals to know they did not take kindly to condescension. "Vick is a wart," he said to the mirror by way of apology. "Please stop the Blood Court!"

The couplet was short and terrible, but it seemed to appease the mirror, which re-solidified without warning. Thankfully, Lizinia had managed to snatch her hand back before losing her fingers.

"The steps we came down are back that way." Vick indicated the shadows to his right.

"This way it is, then," said Trix. Wisdom's tooth brightened around his neck in confirmation.

In silence they descended, down and down, at least twice as far as they'd come from the surface and further still.

"How far down are we going?" asked Trix. "To the center of the world?"

"I imagine we'll stop when the stairs stop," said Lizinia.

"That's the idea," said Vick.

Something in the walls always seemed to be glowing: gems, lichen, pebbles, mushrooms—at times, fine grains twinkled like stars in the rich, dark earth. Trix got dizzy when the staircase spiraled. Eventually, the floor leveled out and there were no more steps to take. It was here where the corridors began. The passages looked incredibly narrow; Trix worried about his uncle's size.

Trix lifted Wisdom's tooth into the cool air. "Dear Tooth, will this path lead us to the Faerie Queen?"

The tooth brightened without hesitation, but its light was muted. It flickered briefly, as if it were a candle about to go out. The sheer pressure of the earth above them seemed to smother everything.

"Welcome to the catacombs," Vick said with false cheer. "A bit like being buried alive, isn't it?"

"Remind me never to get imprisoned while in Faerie," said Lizinia.

Thankfully, the corridor soon widened enough that Trix could walk beside Bear comfortably. He placed his hand casually on his uncle's back and smoothed the fur there, as much to comfort his uncle as it was to give himself courage for the rest of the journey. The angry scratches on his arm throbbed, his stomach growled like Wolf, and the Faerie Queen chanting in his head was making his brain hurt.

Uncle Bear turned his head into Trix's hand, and their eyes met.

"DANGER. BETRAYAL."

He heard his uncle's words so loud and clear that he tripped over his own feet and went sprawling.

"Trix!" Lizinia knelt by his side. "Are you all right?"

"I'm fine." Trix could *feel* his uncle's intentions, stronger than the words he'd spoken. Something was very wrong down here. "I just tripped. Sorry. It's dark and..."

"Trix, look." Lizinia pointed to the ground before them, illuminated by the tooth's ever-dimming light. "Bones."

Had they been human, these bones would have been from a toddler. "Maybe a kobold?"

"Might be," said Vick. "Or something worse."

Kobolds caused more mischief than Trix. Those shape changing misfits started fires, poisoned wells, and led children to their deaths. Kobolds were known for cutting men into pieces, roasting them on spits, or boiling them alive. "What's worse than a kobold?" asked Trix.

"Whatever killed the kobold," said Vick. The leprechaun whipped his head around as if he'd heard something. "Douse the light," he ordered.

Trix was confused. If the light needed to go out, wouldn't the tooth, in all its wisdom, have done so already? Trix began to ask why, but Lizinia placed a hand over his mouth and put a finger to her lips. Trix scowled at her, nodded, and placed a hand over the tooth, muffling the light beneath his fingers.

Lizinia dropped her hand, but did not move further down the hall. No one did. As Trix's eyes adjusted, he could make out a bluish purple light emanating from one of the archways. Slowly, he tiptoed toward the light's source, his companions close behind him.

There, on the floor of the catacombs, lay the bodies of the Faerie Queen…and Sorrow.

11

The Magic Game

rix released Wisdom's tooth and leapt through the archway. "Don't let her speak!"

"Which one?" asked Lizinia.

Vick, who knew the Faerie Queen, fell to his knees beside Sorrow's body and clamped a hand over her mouth. "Not that she's in any shape to be speaking," said the leprechaun. "She's unconscious. They both are."

"She's stolen Mama Woodcutter's power," said Trix. "Every word that passes her lips will find a way to come true. I'm not taking any chances. Lizinia,"—Trix turned to the golden girl—"meet Aunt Sorrow."

"She really does look like your Aunt Joy, doesn't she?"

"Sorrow and Joy are twins," said Trix. "That tends to happen."

Lizinia turned her head to the other woman on the floor. "But she looks a lot like the Faerie Queen too. I'm not sure I would have been able to tell them apart."

"May I?" With Lizinia's permission, Trix used his golden dagger slice up more of her magicked gown. The material parted easily beneath his blade. "The stories say that those blessed with the most fey magic take on the features of the reigning Faerie Queen. Black hair, pale skin…and though you can't tell now, both of their eyes are that haunting shade of indigo."

"Like your sister," said Lizinia. "Wednesday."

Trix sheathed his dagger and used the long pink strips to bind and gag Sorrow. "One day Wednesday will be more powerful than all of them put together." When he finished, Trix stood and looked down at the body of the woman who had caused his family so much pain. "I should kill her."

"Trix, no," said Lizinia.

"Why not?" asked Trix. "She's only going to cause more trouble—if not here, then somewhere else. And my family will suffer for it every time." His hand fell to the dagger at his belt. If he killed Sorrow, her spells would be broken. They could find the fey magic and free it without having to watch their backs. Mama and all of her sisters would wake…or they would die.

There was just one problem.

"You're right. I can't." His hand slipped off the dagger and he clenched his fist. "If Saturday were here, she could do it. She killed that witch in the White Mountains to save the world. She could kill this one."

Save us, Trix Woodcutter, the Faerie Queen chanted in his head. *Save us all.*

"You are not Saturday." Lizinia took his hand so that he would stop hurting himself. "And that is okay."

From behind them, a soft voice beckoned. "Do it."

Bear growled, but if in surprise or warning Trix knew not. The Faerie Queen had managed only to lift her head from the floor to speak the terrible command. She blinked several times and her wan pallor took on a greenish tint.

Lizinia's skirts of gold and tattered pink pooled as she knelt to aid her. "Slowly, your majesty."

"Kill her before she can create any more chaos." The Faerie Queen clung to Lizinia's golden sleeve. The black spot there winked at Trix, reminding him of all the things he'd done wrong in his life up to this point. The Faerie Queen really should have chosen a more reliable champion. Either of his older brothers would have been far more suitable.

"*I can't.*" Trix's words dripped with pain and remorse.

"In the end, you will." The queen's eyes rolled back into her head and she went limp once more.

Trix balled his hands into fists as his sides. Uncle Bear moved in behind him, a good thing in case Trix's legs refused to hold him up any more.

"Trix," said Lizinia. "Today, right now, this is not the end."

Vick took the opportunity to asses the situation. "The binding of the fey magic has incapacitated her. Just like your aunts."

"Even worse than Aunt Joy," said Lizinia. "Which makes sense, since the queen's fey magic would be the strongest and the purest, right?"

Trix's brow furrowed as he tried to work it all out. "Sorrow would have known that binding the fey magic would have overwhelmed the Faerie Queen, and then herself."

Lizinia caught on. "So whatever vessel she used to contain the fey magic is in this room."

"Too bad that vessel's not as easy to find as this one." The leprechaun picked up the Faerie Queen's scepter. As he did, the light in Wisdom's tooth flickered and went out.

"Your timing today is terrible." Trix scowled at the tooth.

The Faerie Queen's scepter glowed in the darkness. Undulating waves of blue and purple and deep, forest green washed over them. Trix and Lizinia stepped closer to the crystal. Uncle Bear kept his distance. The colors tinted his white fur and set his eyes flashing, shifting him from a giant beast into a strange monster of the dream realm. Trix took on a similar hue, but Lizinia's skin turned from gold to black.

"It's like the Dragon Lights," said Trix.

"You mean the sky after the lightning," agreed Lizinia, "when the ocean fled. But those colors shone bright and full of energy. This feels sick. Or poisoned."

Mesmerized, Trix watched the thick, oily fog that was an evil king slide in and around itself beneath the crystal. "There was so much smoke when King Hargath died," Trix marveled. "Amazing that Wednesday and Aunt Joy managed to squeeze it all into something so small."

"Magic," said Lizinia.

"So what do we do now?" asked Vick.

The Faerie Queen's words weren't bouncing around in his head anymore, but Trix's body suddenly felt compelled beyond anything he could control. He wanted to touch the crystal. He *needed* to. He stretched his finger out to the scepter.

"Should you be doing that?" Lizinia stopped Trix's hand with her own, but not before the smoke inside had shifted like a snake, or a cat, recoiling and hissing at a threat.

Lizinia leaned in and peered at the crystal. "There's something in there."

Vick leaned in too. "I wouldn't touch it. You might foul up the spell."

"Wednesday and Aunt Joy wouldn't have gone to all that trouble to trap the king's spirit with a spell that could be broken just by touching it," said Trix.

Lizinia backed up a pace and pulled Trix with her. "But if anyone could break a spell by looking at it sideways, it would be a Woodcutter."

"Go on then," Vick goaded. "We'll brace ourselves."

Trix stretched his finger out to the crystal once more. The smoke writhed, black and purple, black and blue, black and green, faster and faster, as if it could somehow run from Trix's advancing appendage. Trix touched the crystal—it felt cool, despite the dazzling light display. The smoke reared back, fleeing to the opposite side of the faceted ball.

There, in the middle of the crystal, was the true source of its light: a small, glittering star. Now free of the smoke that obscured it, it burned defiant and white, illuminating the catacombs like a tiny sun. As the light touched the Faerie Queen she woke again.

So did Sorrow. Her eyes snapped open and she gasped into her gag. She immediately thrashed against her bonds and moaned noisily.

"It's no more than you deserve," the Faerie Queen said to her attacker. The magic light had roused her, but her voice was still weak.

Bear began to growl. "*DANGER,*" Trix heard his uncle say again.

Sorrow screamed against the gag, long and hard, again and again.

"If she keeps that up, she might pass out," said Lizinia.

"Let her," said Vick.

Trix removed his finger from the crystal and the evil king's smoke swallowed the star inside its oily fog. Sorrow immediately silenced and slumped back to the floor. Within moments, the Faerie Queen had done the same. Blue and purple and green danced across the walls once more.

"Sorrow trapped the fey magic *here,*" said Trix.

"With *him,*" added Lizinia.

"So his bilious soul could hide it from us," said Vick. "But you were too clever, my boy."

"Sorrow was clever first," said Lizinia. "If we break the crystal and release the magic, then the evil king is released as well."

Trix picked up the scepter. "Then we take it back to Wednesday. She helped make the spell. She'll know what to do."

Vick sighed and looked back down the hall. "Isn't there some way to end this right here? I don't relish the idea of wading through the Blood Court a third time."

Lizinia pointed to the scepter. "Will that hold them back?"

"That magic is all they want," said Vick. "What's to stop them from smashing it to pieces the moment they catch wind of what's inside?"

"Her," Trix gently lifted the body of the Faerie Queen. "She's their queen. The court must obey her."

"Or eat her," Vick said out of the corner of his mouth. Trix resisted the urge to kick him.

"I just hope you're right," Lizinia said to Trix.

"I'm not always right." Trix grinned proudly. "But it has been known to happen a time or two."

Lizinia sliced up more of her skirt, and they used the material to secure the unconscious women onto Bear's back. Trix's uncle seemed dubious about the idea, but was willing to give it a try. A lucky thing too; they wouldn't have much luck dragging the two of them up all those stairs, and no one liked the idea of leaving either of them alone in the catacombs.

When they reached the backside of the magic mirror, Trix blew out a breath— his elbow still throbbed where the black-haired man's nails had left their mark. He stepped up to the glass and tested it. Just as it had the first time, the magic barrier allowed Trix's finger to pass right through from this side with no silly rhyming. Hungry members of the Blood Court gathered beyond, aimlessly milling about the ballroom.

"Adventure awaits," Trix whispered to himself before stepping through.

The Blood Court sensed them at once. Whether it was the presence of the Faerie Queen, Trix's blood, or the scepter in his hands that drew them, it didn't matter. Bear broke into a run as soon as they stepped through the mirror's frame. Trix tried not to look at the sickly blue/green/purple light, undulating around them as they raced across the floor behind him.

As Vick suspected, the swirling colors seemed to renew the Blood Court's vigor, and they attacked accordingly.

Bear snarled and bucked, sending men sprawling on either side of him. Lizinia flanked Bear, punching and kicking with all her might. Vick stood away from them, far enough that the four men and women surrounding him had a chance to overwhelm him. Trix, too, had his hands full. With his dagger in one hand and the Faerie Queen's scepter in the other he faced three of them: two of the women that had attacked them the first time, and the black-haired courtier.

The man seemed entranced by the scepter, swaying to the right and left. Trix almost didn't notice the other two lunge at him—it was easier to step towards the black-haired man to avoid their collision than it was to step away. The man took a swing and Trix ducked low. Too low. Before he could regain his footing the three of them had thrown their bodies on top of him.

The black-haired man batted at the scepter, wrenching it out of Trix's grasp, but Trix was not about to let it go willingly. He thrashed against the bodies smothering his as best he could, fighting to keep his hold on the crystal-topped staff. His fingers sought purchase among the decorative vines down its length, but his palms began to sweat as he struggled. The black-haired man was finally able to wrest it from him, but Trix's flailing body sent the scepter flying in a great arc over the floor.

"No!" Trix cried.

He might have heard Lizinia's cry as well, but not Vick's. Had the Blood Court overtaken the leprechaun? Trix tried to follow the scepter as it soared over the heads of the Blood Court, dragging his attackers with him. He could not afford to loose the spirit of the evil king yet. Wednesday needed to be there…was that her at the far end of the ballroom, surrounded by birds? Yes, it was Wednesday! If only she was close enough to catch the scepter…

…but she was not. The staff clattered to the floor at Wednesday's feet.

The crystal had not broken.

Wednesday winked at Trix as she picked up the scepter and walked toward him. Trix exhaled. The black-haired man used the distraction to land a punch in Trix's stomach. His teeth were suddenly dangerously close to Trix's neck.

Lizinia pulled the man's body off of Trix and tossed it in Wednesday's direction. Wednesday spun the scepter around and used the pointed end to stab the man in the abdomen. His body collapsed to the floor this time and did not rise again.

"Trix, here!" Wednesday had brought their bows and arrows with her. Trebald and Aunt Joy and a host of other animals poured into the room. Together, the birds, rabbits, deer, and all the other people-turned-animals under the Hill overwhelmed the Blood Court and turned the tide.

Trix cut the makeshift straps that held Sorrow and the Faerie Queen onto Bear's back and Lizinia helped distribute the pink material to everyone with opposable thumbs. "Tie them up," he said, indicating the Blood Court, and his order was quickly followed.

Wednesday, with the scepter, stood over the bodies of Sorrow and the Faerie Queen, looking for all the world like a queen herself.

"The crystal didn't break," said Trix.

"It's not meant to," said Wednesday. "Ever."

"Ever is a very long time," said Lizinia.

Wednesday shrugged.

Trix looked around the room once more, scanning the occupants. The overlapping murmurs of animal-speak in his head was so overwhelming that he could make out very little of it. He still could not "hear" Uncle Bear fully...and someone else's voice was noticeably absent from the crowd.

"Where's Vick?" Trix asked Lizinia.

"The last I saw he'd taken on four of the Blood Court," said Trix.

"Oh, no," said Lizinia.

"We'll find him," said Wednesday. "Have heart."

Trix hung his head. He had heart, but not much hope. Vick had saved them in the Wood. He'd snuck them under the Hill. He'd fed them their last meal. And now there was every possibility that Vick had given his life for their quest. The ultimate sacrifice. Trix had repaid the leprechaun with nothing but doubt and disdain, all because Papa's stories said that leprechauns could not be trusted.

Trebald tugged on Trix's pant leg with his pointed teeth. "I'll find the scamp," he said. "For you. Yes, yes." With that, the brownie scurried off into the busy ballroom.

Trix forced his mind back on more pressing matters. "Sorrow trapped the Fey magic inside the scepter with Hargath. You have to find something else to trap his wicked spirit inside so we can set the Hill back to rights."

For the first time in any history Trix could remember, Wednesday actually looked frightened. "Even if I found a way to break an unbreakable crystal, I can't manage any of the rest without Aunt Joy."

The aunt in question had curled up next to Bear and looked for all the world like she had fallen asleep. Trix had never seen Joy and Sorrow together in the same room before. Had Sorrow not been bound and gagged, Trix would never have been able to tell them apart. Joy, Sorrow, Wednesday, the Faerie Queen…as soon as they figured out how to release the fey magic, no room would be big enough to contain the combined power of the magic wielded by these four women.

"You can do it," he said to Wednesday. "I believe in you. I always have."

Wednesday swallowed and feigned an air of confidence, even if she did not feel it. "First, I need a vessel," she said.

"Here." Trix held out his dagger. "You said it needed to be something like this or…"

As one, they all turned to Lizinia.

"Or me." She clasped the strap of the star-quiver with both hands. "You said that I was a vessel. Which means the evil king could come into my body and possess me, doesn't it?"

"We would never do that to you," Trix assured her.

"But it's possible," said Wednesday.

Lizinia bit her lips together. It was hard for Trix to get a sense of what she was feeling with all the animal voices in his head. He'd never been so mentally assaulted, even in the thick of the Wood. "What would happen to me then?" Lizinia asked. "The me that is me?"

"The soul that is you and the soul that is Hargath would fight for that body," said Wednesday.

"She could fight him," said Trix.

"She would lose," said Wednesday. "I'm sorry, but it's true. Hargath is too powerful."

"No," said Lizinia defiantly. "I choose to stay and fight." She turned to Trix. "Vick gave his life for this. How could I do any less?"

She lifted the rain-bow and extracted a star arrow from the quiver. "I will break the crystal with the gods' arrow, and you"—she looked to Wednesday—"will trap that evil king's soul in Trix's dagger."

"We need something to prop up the scepter," said Trix. He removed his vest and shirt, making a pile of them some distance away from Bear and the rest of the crowd in the ballroom. Beside the pile he placed his golden dagger. Then he returned to retrieve the scepter from Wednesday.

As he passed by the Faerie Queen, her eyelids fluttered open and she mumbled something at him. He leaned in to hear her, but she slumped unconscious again. Trix looked to the bound Blood Court, decided it was safe enough, and touched the crystal with his finger. The black smoke fled to the opposite side of the crystal, and the star of fey magic alit upon the pale face of the Faerie Queen. She smiled into the light before opening her indigo eyes once more.

"You will smash that crystal, Trix Woodcutter. You will save the fey magic this day. I am proud to have chosen you as my Emissary."

"You made me your Emissary to talk to the animals, your majesty, but I feel that I have failed you. I was only able to communicate with a few under this Hill. I couldn't even talk to my uncle."

The Faerie Queen's wan smile grew wider. "That's not why I brought you here."

"Then why?"

"You, Trix Woodcutter, were my pawn. You set the pieces in motion and you brought us all here, to the end of my game."

Trix didn't mind being an Emissary, but he didn't like the idea of being anyone's pawn. "I'm not playing a game."

"Of course you're not," said the Faerie Queen. "It is my game. In this game, I am the only one who wins."

"Trix!" Lizinia called. "What is taking you so long? Is the queen all right?"

The queen, Trix surmised, was addle-brained from lack of magic. "Excuse me," said Trix.

The Faerie Queen caught him by the trouser leg with a surprisingly strong hand. "You *will* break the crystal in that staff," she said in a melodious voice. Trix's eyes widened in horror. He knew that voice. It was the voice Mama Woodcutter used when she gave an order she knew would be obeyed.

"No!" Trix cried out. "It's not the Faerie Queen! It's Sorrow!"

"You will break that crystal," she said as Lizinia flew across the ballroom. "And you will free my lover."

Lizinia clapped a hand over the false queen's mouth before she could say any more, but it was too late. Somehow, Sorrow had swapped bodies with the Faerie Queen. And she had stolen Mama Woodcutter's power, so now her every word would find a way to come true.

Unable to stop himself, Trix removed his finger from the crystal, clasped the scepter by its base, and began slamming the crystal into the floor, over and over again.

"Trix, what are you doing?" yelled Lizinia.

"She told me I had to break the crystal!" he yelled back.

"Then at least hold it up so I can hit it with an arrow!"

"You can't break the crystal," he said. "She told me *I* have to be the one." He kept hammering the floor with the scepter, even though he knew it would accomplish nothing. He couldn't tell his body to stop. The crystal cracked the floor, but it did not break. Trix crossed the room, pounding floor, columns, and walls with no end in sight.

"Not the mirror!"

Lizinia's cry wouldn't have been able to stop him. There was no time to drum up a clever rhyme. Crystal met glass, and with a great crash the magic mirror shattered.

Framed in the secret tunnel beyond was Vick, standing over the severed head of Old Sassy.

Trix and Lizinia—who had caught up to him—both screamed at the sight. Vick fled into the shadows. Somewhere in the distance, a wolf answered their cry. Lizinia found her wits before Trix did. She wrenched the scepter from his hands and tossed it over to where the pile of clothes and the dagger lay.

"You can break it," she said with intensity, as if her command might break through the geis compelling him. "In your hands, your bow is as magic as mine." They made their stances, raised their bows, and drew together. Trix could not let her shoot first. He had to be the one to break that crystal. Sorrow had said so, and so it must be done.

Perhaps Lizinia intended to shoot Vick for the murder of their dear friend…but Trix couldn't concentrate on that. He couldn't concentrate on anything but the feel of the bow in his hands, the pull of the string beneath his chin, the brush of the fletch against his fingers. The scepter, even at such a distance, appeared to him in perfect focus. The smoke in the crystal swirled with anticipation.

A wild roar filled Trix's head, but it was not Bear.

Wolf.

Wolf barreled down the secret stair, ready to kill them all with teeth and claws and speed a thousandfold more dangerous than the Blood Court. Trix would deal with that, but first he had to smash this crystal. He fired his shot, and missed. Lizinia's bowstring remained taut.

"No!" Trix cried, and quickly grabbed another arrow.

Lizinia turned, and they both fired.

Trix's arrow found the crystal.

Lizinia's arrow found Wolf's heart.

The ballroom around them exploded.

12

The Star

There were no animal voices in his mind, only a steady, high pitched tone that muffled everything else beneath it.

Trix took in a breath, happy to still be able to do so. His chest ached, though any pain he felt seemed to be centered at the base of his skull and in his right arm—the spasming muscles gave no sign that they were ready to relax.

The floor was cold. The air smelled of lightning and singed hair and...cherries?

Trix blinked his eyes. They felt sticky and dry. His nose and mouth were too, as if the explosion had sucked all of the dampness out of the underground atmosphere.

Explosion.

The fey magic. King Hargath. Wolf. Sassy. Vick. Sorrow.

There were so many things Trix needed to think about right

now that his fuzzy brain refused to process any of them.

He reached out for Lizinia. She wasn't there. Hadn't she been right beside him when he fell?

Trix summoned his strength and rolled onto his right side. His head swam, and he resisted the familiar urge to vomit. All too familiar. He remembered feeling the same after being tossed about on a particular magical ocean.

Magic.

Trix groaned.

Magic would be the death of the Woodcutters.

He pushed himself up—both arms were in pain, it seemed, but only one was frozen—and slowly turned his head. There were bodies everywhere. He hoped they were alive. As he forced himself to his feet it occurred to him: these were human bodies, or human-ish. All of them. The fey magic had returned the animal-blooded members of the court back to their regular forms.

Most of them were naked. A few of them might care about that when they woke.

Unfortunately that subject was low on Trix's list of priorities.

He needed to fetch that dagger and he had to wake Wednesday and Aunt Joy. *Immediately*.

Trix clasped his right arm with his left hand, ordering it to stop jumping beneath his skin so that he could better concentrate on putting one foot in front of the other without falling down. Where was Aunt Joy? He had last seen her with Uncle Bear. But Uncle Bear was no longer an actual bear now, and thus considerably more difficult to spot in a crowd of randomly strewn fairy folk.

The ringing in his ears diminished a bit and Trix could make out a moan or two from the bodies he passed. Some on the fringes of the ballroom stood and quietly stumbled away, presumably to regain their bearings in familiar surroundings…and to clothe themselves.

There. To his left. A large man with alabaster skin and silver hair, large enough that Trix could still imagine him as a bear. Beside the large man lay three women of the same age and coloring. Two were bound with pink sashes. One was not.

Aunt Joy.

Trix tried to walk to her and immediately tumbled to the floor. He turned back to unhook his foot from the crook of a body's elbow.

The body of the black-haired courtier…dead no more.

As if Trix's contact had shook him awake, the corpse opened his eyes. They were no longer ruby red.

Nor were they soulless.

The irises of the dead man's eyes swirled black, with flashes of blue and green and purple as the light hit them.

Hargath's spirit hadn't found Trix's dagger, nor had it sought out Lizinia—where *was* she?—to use as a host. The evil king's wretched soul had found a new host. The dead man's empty body had been ripe for the taking

The man that was now Hargath shot up to a sitting position and stood, stiffly, as if actions such as sitting and standing and walking were unfamiliar to him. He made a beeline for Sorrow—the true body of Sorrow that Trix hoped was not still inhabited by the soul of the Faerie Queen. Hargath shoved bodies out of the way, stepping on a few as he passed. He bent and lifted Sorrow into his arms. She was still bound and, blessedly, unconscious.

Trix got to his hands and knees and scrambled over to Aunt Joy. "Please wake up." He shook her. "Please!" He patted her cheeks. He pinched her. "Please, Aunt Joy, hurry! They're getting away!" Speaking was painful as his voice echoed sharply inside his skull, but he forced himself to push through it.

Trix looked around for a weapon. He'd left his bow and quiver by the mirror, and his golden dagger remained by the pile of clothes where the scepter had been. Trix had magic within himself, but even if he knew how to summon it, it would not be enough to stop Sorrow and her consort.

As Hargath approached the mirror, Trix gave up on Aunt Joy and switched to the Faerie Queen. Or whom he hoped was the Faerie Queen. He took the risk of removing her gag and bindings, shaking her and pleading all the while. "Get up," he cried. "Please, get up! I can't do this alone!"

"You are never alone, little brother."

Trix cried out at the sound of Saturday's voice.

"They're getting away, Saturday! Hurry!"

She and Peregrine crossed the sea of shattered mirror. They were followed by a large rabbit-like animal with even larger antlers. "Who's getting away?" asked his warrior sister.

Trix scanned the room from there Wednesday had entered to the darkness of the cave beyond the mirror. Nothing. Defeated, he plopped down on his bottom. "Sorrow."

"So our evil aunt was here," said Saturday. "Figures."

"Where's Lizinia?" asked Peregrine.

"I haven't found her yet," said Trix. "It's possible she went to fetch some clothes."

Saturday looked puzzled. "But she doesn't need clothes, right?"

"Right." Trix smiled. "But just about everyone else here does." The rabbit peeked out from behind Peregrine and moved to scratch his fuzzy antlers on the nearest pillar. "Is that a jackalope?"

"It's Betwixt," said Saturday. "I'll explain later."

Saturday's clothes were in tatters. Angry red scratches covered her cheeks and chest and arms and legs, all of them parallel, like the claws of a wolf. She wore the remnants of a torn shirt tied above her left elbow. And around her right thigh. Peregrine didn't look much better.

Before the White Mountains, all of Saturday's wounds would have been healed by now. Now that his sister had found her destiny—presumably killing the witch...or freeing the dragon...or finding Peregrine—she was considerably worse for the wear.

Trix made a show of examining her injuries. "Getting old."

Saturday's wry grin said that she was too tired to punch her little brother. "I'm more worried about Peregrine's pretty face."

Peregrine adjusted the makeshift bandage around his temples. "Scars add character."

Saturday chuckled. "You're enough of a character without them."

"I'm so glad you're here," Trix said, relieved. "You found my mark on the silver birch?"

"That's what took us so long." Saturday smirked. "I assumed you hadn't just waked in the front door, but there was a "T" on almost every tree from here to Arilland. Did you run afoul of a leprechaun?"

"'Afoul' is putting it kindly," said Trix. He took back anything nice he'd even considered thinking about Vick.

Members of the Faerie Court began to return to the ballroom with piles of blankets and various items of clothing. The slight wisps—Trix assumed they had been the birds—wrapped long scarves around themselves artfully. A bunny in a multicolor tunic—Trix couldn't decide if he was a page or a jester—hopped about on his two hind legs, frenetically seeing to this and that with the haste of someone who is constantly in a panic about something.

"Where has she gone?" The commanding voice was not that of the Faerie Queen but Aunt Joy, now fully back to her senses. Wednesday, on the other hand, had returned to her blissful, magic-muddled, half-present state. She had swathed herself in wisp scarves and was dancing about the room, weaving in and out around bodies as they woke.

And Saturday had missed it completely. Only Trix and Lizinia and Trebald would remember Wednesday as the woman she might have been. Trix's heart hurt.

And his stomach growled.

"Hargath possessed the body of the dead courtier and stole Sorrow away," Trix summed up plainly. "I didn't have the strength to stop them alone. I'm so sorry."

Aunt Joy shook her head. "That was the wisest course, young man. With all the power at her disposal right now, I'm not sure even I could have stopped my twin sister alone."

Trix shivered, even as the muscle of his right arm spasmed again. It was a dreadful thought. "Sorrow *was* the Faerie Queen," he said. "I know she stole my birthmother's gift of disguise, but this went far beyond that. Sorrow's spirit completely took over a body that was not her own."

"Spirit magic." The answer came from Uncle Bear, now clad in trousers too short for his long legs. "It is the gift of my wife, Snow White." In human form, Uncle Bear was taller and wider and maybe even stronger than Papa, characteristics that made Trix both envious and homesick all at the same time.

"The Faerie Queen came to me in a vision and summoned me here to the Hill," said Trix. "But it wasn't the Faerie Queen at all, was it?"

"It was not I who came to you."

Everyone in earshot of those words bowed and curtseyed to the Faerie Queen.

"Your majesty," said Trix, Saturday, and Peregrine.

"Corinna," said Aunt Joy.

Uncle Bear quickly knelt and helped her sit up. "I did not know you to send for you, Trix Woodcutter, but I will be eternally grateful that you came." Her eyes scanned the family before her. "I thank all of you for bringing the fey magic back into the world. We owe you our lives."

"It could have gone a lot better," Trix mumbled

"Most things that happen in this life could always turn out better," said the Faerie Queen. "But it also might have been a lot worse."

Uncle Bear's reassuring hand was so large that it swallowed Trix's shoulder. "This is not over," said Bear. "We live to fight another day. I, for one, will not stop until my wife is freed from Sorrow's spell."

"If anyone is to blame, it is me, child," said Aunt Joy. "I am my sister's keeper."

"A job no one gave you, but one that you have taken upon yourself regardless," said the Faerie Queen. "I blame you only for being bullheaded and loyal, my dearest goddaughter. Only a fool would blame a person for the actions of someone else."

Trix smiled. Aunt Joy was godmother to the Woodcutter siblings, but he had never considered that Mama and her sisters would have had a godmother as well. It made sense, as close as their grandfather had been to the Faerie Queen, that her majesty would be the fey guardian of the Mouton sisters.

This was the only way in which Trix was not a true Woodcutter—Aunt Joy had never given him a nameday gift, as she had with all his foster brothers and sisters. Not that it mattered to him, really. Trix was a Woodcutter sibling in so many other ways.

"Forgive me," the Faerie Queen said to Trix. "I don't feel that I have the right to ask anything more of you, dear boy, but...what happened here?"

It wasn't a strange question; she'd been bound and gagged and unconscious for most of the time. Trying to put the answer into words, however, was tougher than it should have been. Voices and magic and memories were still a jumble in Trix's spinning head

Trix screwed up his nose as he tried to remember everything in the right order. "I was placing the scepter on the pile so Lizinia could shoot at it with her magic arrows and try to destroy it, when Sorrow—I thought she was you, your majesty—stopped me. She commanded me to break the crystal immediately. Me, not Lizinia. I had no choice but to do my best and I smashed everything with it"—he gasped—"including your magic mirror! I'm so sorry."

The Faerie Queen waved his apology away. "Think nothing of it. I will ask the dwarves to make me another one."

Any other day, Trix would have been stymied by the fact that he'd broken an enormous, sacred, possibly ancient object and not gotten in trouble for it, but not this day. "Vick was back there and—oh! He killed Old Sassy!"

"Who's Vick?" asked Saturday.

"The filthy leprechaun," said Trix.

"That dear horse," said Peregrine.

"Lizinia was with me when we saw what happened to Sassy," said Trix. "She was very angry. She drew her bow, but I couldn't let her break the crystal. I had to be the one to break it. Sorrow compelled me. Lizinia shot…Wolf! He attacked us, and she shot Wolf! Oh, no."

In a heartbeat, Bear leapt up and crossed the room to where the mirror had been. Trix, fueled by the anxiety of his memories, was close behind.

Poor Sassy's severed head still sprawled gorily across the threshold from the once-hidden cavern into the ballroom. Just past her nose, face down on the stone, was a man.

Trix tilted his head the way Lizinia always did (where *was* she? He was beginning to worry). The man lay where Wolf had fallen, but this body was not the one Trix had expected. This was not the hirsute companion that had traveled with them on the road. This man was fully human. His long hair was thick and had the same multicolored attributes, but he was far less fuzzy from head to toe, and thus seemed far slighter. Beneath the now-sparse hairs Trix could make out the cords of his strong muscles, well-defined beneath his light brown skin.

It was easy for Trix to believe that a wolf had muscles like that. Could it really be Wolf? Why would the fey magic have changed him so drastically?

Saturday tossed a blanket to Bear. He thanked her for it, covering his friend before turning him over. Wolf's face was now as human as any of the fey now staring down at him. His eyes were closed; long lashes brushed his cheeks. Despite the mass of hair on his head, he was clean shaven. Even his eyebrows seemed thinner.

There was also no wound on his breast where Lizinia's magic arrow had pierced his heart, only a many-pointed star the size and shade of a gold coin. Bear hung his head, silver hair falling over his face to hide his torment. He placed one large hand on his friend's lifeless body, right over that star.

Bear growled deep in his chest—the words that followed were not the prayer Trix was expecting. "This is not how it's supposed to be."

Apparently, Fate agreed.

Wolf turned his head and his chest rose ever so slightly.

Trix stepped back as friends and family surged in to assess Wolf's state, the Faerie Queen among them. Trix took the opportunity to scan the ballroom crowd again for Lizinia. Even in the tumult, the golden girl should have been easy to spot.

"Lizinia!" he cried out for good measure, but there was no answer. "Where have you gone?" he whispered more to himself than anyone.

"He took her," said a voice. "Wretched leprechaun. Bad news, the lot of them."

Trix spun around, but the only people close to him were the ones worrying over Wolf. "Who said that?"

"Down here."

Surely it couldn't have been...

Trix bent himself in half and stared into the fixed eyes of Sassy's severed head. "Sassy?"

The horse blinked.

"Oh, Sassy! It *is* you!"

Saturday snapped to attention at Trix's exclamation and she rushed over. "What on earth?"

"Sassy's alive!" Trix cried. "Isn't it wonderful?" The news made him so giddy he wanted to dance.

"I admit, it would be more wonderful if I had a body," said Sassy.

"Whoa." Saturday shook her head. "I heard that! Sassy, I heard you! And incidentally, I agree."

"Heavens." Peregrine was the next to join them. "Did the fey magic do this?"

"It makes sense," said Trix. "Sassy, are you all right?" Well of course she wasn't all right. She had no body to speak of, and could only look in whatever direction she was pointed. Trix attempted his question again, with a higher degree of sensitivity. "I mean...are you in any pain?"

The horse shifted her eyes from side to side, as if considering the question. "I don't think so," she said finally. "I can't really feel anything, except maybe a slight tickle on the left side of my nose."

Trix addressed the tickle promptly. It was the least he could do.

"What's this about Lizinia?" asked Peregrine.

"Where *is* Lizinia?" asked Saturday. "Did she run off with the queen's bees?"

"Vick took her," said Trix. Trebald had gone after Vick. If the brownie could lead Trix to the leprechaun, he could find Lizinia...

"Yes! That's what I'm trying to tell you," said Sassy. "Vick hid himself down among the rocks before the fairy crystal exploded, so he wasn't overwhelmed like the rest of you. He waited until everyone went down and stayed down, and then he dragged Lizinia out the back stair."

"He must be considerably stronger than he looks," said Trix.

"You're telling me," said the horse. "While Peregrine and Saturday were off chasing Wolf, Betwixt and I came upon Vick scheming in the Wood. We tried to stop him, but he was too fast for us. Well, for me, anyway." Trix got the impression that if Sassy still had the ability to hang her head, this is when she would have done it. "Vick said your golden girl was his payment for leading all of us—all of you—to Sorrow. I suppose he knew that her ultimate goal was to break the crystal."

"And once that was done, he decided not to wait around to collect," said Saturday. "Typical leprechaun."

"He was incredibly proud of himself about the whole thing."

"Slimy little bugaboo," said Trix. "I always knew he had an angle."

"He threw her bow and arrows over there." Sassy's eyes rolled back toward the cave—Trix searched the steps and the rocks until he found the rain-bow and quiver of star arrows. He gave them both a small hug before settling them into place next to his own bow and quiver. If Lizinia had been unconscious then Vick couldn't have gotten far. Or could he?

Exactly how long *had* they all been awake? Blast the Hill for not having any windows to the outside world. Granted, that's probably something the magic mirror had been used for. Before he'd gone and smashed it.

"Hello there, Sassy!" Bear's timbre rang out as he addressed the horse's head on the floor. "Remember me?"

Sassy's muzzle wrinkled. "I lost my body, not my nose, silly Bear. I can still smell you a mile away. Now, tell me what happened to Wolf. Don't sugar coat it. I'm an old mare. I can take it."

"It seems you can," said Bear. "But not to worry. Apart from a desperately needed molting, Wolf seems to be fine. We'll have a better idea when he wakes. They're taking him back to my room—he can't tell us otherwise, but I expect it's more comfortable than this floor. What say you, Sassy? Would you like to come along?"

Sassy sniffed and whuffled. "Will Your Stinkyness be the one carrying me there?"

"I would entrust this very important task to no other," said Bear. Saturday and Peregrine hid their smiles back where Sassy couldn't see them. Trix's uncle scooped Sassy's head up and propped it gently over his shoulder. "Come on, nephew," he said. "Time for everyone to get cleaned up and sorted out."

Trix didn't want to clean himself up or sort himself out. He wanted to race up those stairs and out the secret entrance to the Hill and find Lizinia *immediately*. The trouble was, he had no idea how. For now, he had to trust in Trebald. And Lizinia. She was so much like his sisters: clever to a fault and strong, inside and out. He wouldn't be surprised if she'd already gotten the best of Vick and was headed back right this moment.

Trix frowned. Well, if she hadn't yet, surely she would soon.

He gathered up his dagger, the bows, and his foul mood and fell in behind the queen's entourage now exiting the ballroom. Sassy, facing backwards over Bear's shoulder, had no choice but to stare directly at Trix and his sour expression. "Chin up, young one," she said. "You will find your golden girl."

"I hope so," he said without much hope at all.

"Have heart," the horse told him cheerfully. "One of us has to."

13

The Champions

"I know that face."

It took Trix a moment to register that Peregrine had said anything at all. They sat together in the hot pools of the bath caverns, the place to which the Faerie Queen's Champions had been ordered until fresh clothes and supplies could be readied for them.

The old Trix would have splashed about in the great pools, dove deep to see what gems he could scoop up from beneath the warm, crystal clear waters, and sung at the top of his lungs so that his happiness might echo off the high, arched ceilings all the way to the women's bathing chambers. This Trix was tired. For the first time in his life, maybe. He was tired of being sent on fool's errands.

Trix did not lift his head from where it rested on his arms at the edge of the pool. His scratches had faded, but all the aches were still there. "What face is that?"

"The one where you wish you could run off to find your companion and resume your own travels on your own time," said Peregrine, "but you can't. I saw that face in the mirror at Rose Red Abbey not too long ago. They cleaned us up there, too, after Saturday and Betwixt and I came down from the White Mountain. We went straight from there into other adventures, not entirely of our choosing."

Trix might have felt some guilt at dragging his sister and her new friends on his quest. Knowing the Woodcutters, they would have ended up embroiled in this affair whether they'd followed Trix or not.

"If I must be part of a devious scheme, it should at least be *my* devious scheme," said Trix.

Peregrine rubbed at his temple where Aunt Joy had worked her healing magic. The two pale lines there were all that was left of Wolf's handiwork. "I'll drink to that."

"Just not this water." Trix wrinkled his nose.

"Come now, Trix," said Peregrine. "Where's your sense of adventure? Betwixt doesn't seem to mind it at all."

Trix wished he had been there to see the pegasus change into a jackalope. Betwixt's fur was now patches of white and brown and gray. His antlers were similar patches of the same colors; in some spots fuzzy, in some spots hard as bone. Betwixt did not speak in this form, nor could Trix understand him—he made his feelings known with a severe stomping of his feet in rapid succession or a flick of his tail.

Only the chimera's eyes remained unchanged, flashing that peculiar orange-yellow whenever the light caught them. Hearing his name, the Betwixt glared at Trix and Peregrine before bending down once more to lap at the water.

Trix pulled a face. "Will you tell him he drank that when you can communicate again?"

Peregrine smiled and shrugged. "Maybe. Maybe not."

"All right then, boys, out with you." Uncle Bear's timbre made the crystals in the walls of the cavern hum. "There are things to be getting on with, and we don't want you so shriveled up that we have to alter your clothes."

"Finally," said Trix.

"Duty calls," sighed Peregrine.

They hopped out of the pool and dried off before sorting through the basket of clothes Bear had brought for them. Trix extracted a long garment that looked like a cross between a coat and a dress. "This must be for you," said Trix.

"Thank you," Peregrine said as he took the item, and then pointed to the basket. "You can have that shirt. It seems to be moving."

Trix lifted the shirt to reveal a very confused Trebald. "Hello there, friend!"

The brownie nosed at the sky, his whiskers twitching. "Trix! My goodness, you're so clean I hardly recognized you. No, no."

"It's so good to see you!" Trix's heart soared. "Were you able to find Vick? Was Lizinia with him?"

"He has something he wants to tell you." Uncle Bear said this in the same tone Papa used when he expected Trix to apologize for something.

"Whatever it is, I'm sure it's fine," Trix said in anticipation.

Trebald's whiskers's twitched again. Trix could tell the brownie was trembling from head to toe, so he picked him up and cradled him in one arm. "Truly. Everything will be all right. I promise." Not that anyone could ever truly promise such a thing, but it was still nice to hear from time to time.

"I'm sorry that I didn't see Vick for what he was right away," Trebald said quietly. "Sorry. Yes, yes. I knew he was bad. If I'd known how bad, I would have bitten him directly. Yes, yes."

"We all would have," said Peregrine. "You weren't to know."

"That's not all," said Bear.

"I couldn't find Lizinia," said Trebald. "No, no."

Trix deflated. "That's all right," he said. "Just take me to wherever you lost Vick's trail in the Wood and I'll pick it up from there."

"No, no." Trebald hung his head. "I didn't make it to the Wood."

"Whyever not?" Trix examined the brownie. Was he ill? Was he hurt?

"I ate the berries. Yes, yes."

"What?" Trix turned to Bear. "When Vick said we couldn't eat the food because its magic was wild, he wasn't lying? You're trapped here *forever*?" It was sad enough to lose one traveling companion. Now Trix was about to lose them both.

"Afraid so," said Bear.

"Is the food safe now?" asked Peregrine.

"Aye," said Bear. "The queen's power tempers the Hill's magic. For instance, this pool will heal your wounds, but it won't make everyone who drinks from it immortal."

Peregrine looked over to Betwixt, still drinking his fill, and shrugged.

"Oh, Trebald," said Trix. "Couldn't you have waited?" But he knew the answer. Trix had known that hunger, and he knew Trebald's nervous condition had made the poor brownie feel that same hunger tenfold.

The brownie's cloudy eyes looked askance. "These were difficult days. Yes, yes."

"The queen has promised to make his life here very comfortable," said Bear.

Trebald instantly perked up. "The queen has gifts for all her champions," he said brightly. "Yes, yes. Imagine me, a queen's champion."

"From the Top of the World to the Bottom of the Hill, my friend," said Peregrine.

"We couldn't have done it without you, Trebald," said Trix. "I will miss you every day."

"I will be here when you return," said Trebald. "Yes, yes. Think of all the stories we will have to share."

Trix patted the brownie's head. "We will, indeed," he said, with as much cheer as he could muster in his broken heart. When he left this hallowed hill, he would be traveling alone. Not that he was every truly alone, for the animals of the Wood were always with him, and he had started out on his first quest all by himself. But now that he knew what it was like to share his adventures with others, loneliness loomed.

Loneliness and worry. But Lizinia would be fine. Trix would find her and they would continue their journey to the King of

Eagles. After he kicked that two-faced leprechaun.

"Yes, yes. If you please, Bear." Obligingly, Trix's very large uncle scooped up the very small brownie and lifted him to where he could perch atop his substantial shoulder. "I'm excited to 'see' what my fair queen has in store for the rest of you. Yes, yes."

Trix and Peregrine finished dressing as swiftly as they could. Trix was happy to find a new pair of boots in the basket, his size, made of soft, supple leather but with extremely sturdy soles. Hidden inside one of them was a new belt, with a polished scabbard that fit his golden dagger perfectly. There was also a beautifully crafted bag—if he'd had to guess he would have said it was made from dragon scales. The attached leather thong was just long enough to completely conceal the bag beneath his shirt.

Trix glanced over to where Peregrine was buttoning up his fine coat. He, too, wore a necklace—a golden ring hung from a silver chain. "This might be for you," he said, offering the bag to Peregrine.

Peregrine put a hand over the ring, pressing it against his chest in what looked to Trix like a habitual gesture. "Thank you, but this chain has served me well enough in my adventures. You should keep that for your clever tooth."

Trix mirrored Peregrine's gesture and placed a hand over Wisdom's tooth. He suddenly felt a little less lonely.

⁓❦⁓

Compared to the Great Hall of the Faerie Queen, the ballroom was a privy. The ceiling rose so high that Trix could not even make it out, and the walls were separated by miles. Trix wondered that such a place could exist underground, even with the intricately carved stone support pillars scattered throughout, as there had been in the ballroom. The stone here was all white, accented by clear crystals lit with a magic inner fire that made the whole room glow.

The Hall itself needed no artwork or extravagant decoration, for the population was colorful enough. Trix's heart swelled to see so many people in attendance: members of the court in their finery, some with pointed ears or long tails and some with no visible oddity at all. There were a few tall, gray individuals that reminded Trix of the Spriggans—Trebald told him these were the stonekeepers, whose job was to maintain the Great Pillars of Faerie. There were wisps aplenty, a handful of naiads, and a smattering of faunfolk...Trix could have sworn he had even spotted a Green Child or two among the crowd.

So enraptured was he by the company in their true forms, that he missed the entire beginning of the Faerie Queen's elaborate ceremony. She sat before them on a throne of jewels and thorns, in a dress that looked like ebony spider silk.

"...I can think of no better way to thank these brave souls gathered here before you. My saviors. My champions!"

The assembled crowd's cheer sounded like water and bells and song.

"Saturday Woodcutter, goddaughter of my goddaughter." Saturday stepped forward. She looked far more comfortable in the plain shirt and trousers she'd been given. "To you I give a strand of my hair."

This may have seemed an odd gift, but Trix knew its true power. The blue-green fabric band around Saturday's wrist contained hair from all of her family, even Jack. All but Tuesday, lost these many years to death. Through this link she had the ability to call upon her family members for strength and magic, and give it to them in turn. Though no one would know it, having the Faerie Queen's magic in that mix gave Saturday a mighty weapon.

Saturday bowed to accept the gift and stepped back as Peregrine and Betwixt stepped forward. Unlike Saturday, Peregrine dressed like the great lord he was.

"Peregrine of Starburn. I hear you have a ring."

Peregrine removed his necklace and handed it to the Faerie Queen. She curled her fingers around it and closed her eyes. When her eyes opened again, she smiled. "Your traveling companion has a ring with certain transformative properties," the queen said. "I felt it only right that you should have a weapon to match."

"Thank you, your majesty." Peregrine gave a small bow to the queen and a lusty wink to Saturday before stepping back into place.

"Betwixt." The queen knelt so that she could look the rabbit-deer in the eye. Though he could not speak, Betwixt gave every sign that he understood her words. "As a shapeshifter, it made no sense to give you an object from my court. Instead I will give you the answer to a question so old that you no longer seek it." She lowered her head and whispered in his ear.

Trix could not tell if the chimera smiled, but the queen let Betwixt nuzzle her cheek politely before hopping back beside Peregrine.

"My dearest Wolf," said the queen. "I cannot give you anything more precious than the destiny you already possess." As she said this, she put a hand over his heart where Lizinia's golden star marked the skin beneath his fine clothes. "You journey down your own path, and I would not keep you from it. But I can give you a new steed, from my stables."

"Thank you, my queen."

"I assume you will want to join him, Bear."

Bear's black eyes flashed in the glowing crystal light. "Yes, your majesty."

"And so my gift to you will be the leave to go. Sorrow will be traveling East, to confront Rose Red, and I would not have my Wolf fight alone."

"Nor would I let him, majesty."

"Only promise me that you will come back safely. All of you. That includes Snow White."

Bear bowed low. "I promise."

"Which brings us to you, my dear Falada."

All but Trix turned in surprise as the Queen spoke Sassy's true name. Trix rocked back on his heels and grinned knowingly. The head of Sassy—now Falada—had been groomed and mounted on a thick plaque of polished oak.

"Will I be receiving a new body, mistress?" asked the horse.

The queen patted Falada tenderly. "I would have to separate the head of one of your fellow horses from her body to make it so."

The horse blinked. Tears fell from her sad eyes. "I could not ask that."

"I thought as much," said the Faerie Queen. "And so I will ask something of you instead. It seems that my Spriggans have passed on, and the gate to my Hill finds itself in need of a new guardian. I was wondering if you might oblige? It would require speaking to everyone who passes beneath you, judging them, and notifying me if they are found wanting." The queen folded her hands together. "It is a permanent post, so I'm afraid it would also require you to live far longer than you had previously expected."

Falada snorted. "I've already lived far longer than previously expected. What's a few centuries more? Thank you, my queen."

"Thank *you*, my guardian." The Faerie Queen leaned in and kissed Falada on the forehead. "Now for you, Trix Woodcutter."

Trix swallowed. He'd been on the verge of jumping out of his skin with anticipation of what his gift might be. Now that it was his turn, he wasn't sure he wanted to know. Staring into the queen's depthless indigo eyes made him want to break down and cry. He could not quash the feeling that he had disappointed her somehow, betraying them all by falling into Sorrow's trap and enabling more chaos. There was a time when Trix took pride in his chaos. Losing that was such a shame.

Losing Lizinia was harder.

Perhaps he would be given a choice of gifts? If so, he would ask how to find Lizinia. And what was the fastest way there. And how to defeat the leprechaun. He could weave all that into one wish, he felt sure. Trix brightened at the prospect.

Unexpectedly, Aunt Joy stepped up to stand beside the queen. "My dear Trix. My nephew. My godson, though you never received a nameday gift and never once bemoaned the lack of it. You thrived, despite my shortcomings, and I am so proud of you."

"Shortcomings?" It was odd to think that one of the most powerful women he knew could still fail at something.

"The gift you deserved was not within my power to give." Aunt Joy smiled at the expression of incredulity he could not hide. "Even

I have limits, my boy. But I have discussed it with Corinna, and she has agreed to join her magic with mine so that you might finally have it."

Trix wasn't sure what to say. It wasn't what he would have asked for, but he certainly wasn't going to turn it down, whatever it was. He might have been a rascal, but he was a clever boy for all that.

As it turned out, he didn't need to say anything anyway. Joy and the Faerie Queen clasped hands. The Faerie Queen closed her eyes. There was a deep blue glow between their fingers. The crystals in the walls dimmed and the air smelled like lightning. His aunt reached her free hand up to brush the hair out of his face and, just as the queen had done with Falada, Joy kissed Trix on the forehead.

Trix felt a prickling in the skin all over his body, but that might have been from sweat. The anticipated lightning did not crack into thunder. There was no crash, no boom, no sparkle…nothing. The room brightened as the women separated, but that was all.

Aunt Joy took a step back. "There."

There what? Trix felt nothing. He looked at his hands. They hadn't changed, nor was there anything in them. A thought occurred to him, and he turned to the rest of the champions.

"Do I have a star on my forehead?" Lizinia possessed such a magical star, and Wolf had acquired one by magical means. But the champions squinted at him and shook their heads. Even Falada.

Trix scowled. Aunt Joy chuckled and cupped his cheek with her cool fingers. "Don't worry, my Wild Child. It will manifest when you need it."

Her statement didn't do much to improve his mood. There was

a list of things he could think of that he needed to manifest themselves now, and "ethereal nameday gift" wasn't among them. But Mama had taught him to be gracious in times like this, no matter what the circumstance, so he bowed to his aunt and the queen. "Thank you."

"For my part, I relieve you of the title of my Emissary," said the Faerie Queen, "as it was falsely given. Though I hope you would retain the title of Champion."

It was difficult for Trix not to feel some pride at this. "I will, your majesty."

The buzzing, singing, humming, whistling cheers that followed were beautifully deafening. It was followed by more singing, and dancing, and greetings. The Queen's Champions took the opportunity to embrace each other and bid a few farewells.

"Where will you go?" Trix asked Saturday.

"Back to Arilland," said his warrior sister. "It's past time I went home and made peace with Papa and Peter, and I want Rumbold to consider me for the King's Guard."

"She's still punishing herself for creating that ocean," said Peregrine.

"For Saturday, joining the King's Guard isn't exactly punishment," said Trix.

Saturday punched him in the shoulder, like old times. "Arilland may need an army before all this Sorrow business is said and done. But mostly, I want to take Peregrine and Betwixt to the towerhouse. I want to show them our home."

"I am envious," said Trix. But as much as his sick heart longed for Arilland, he would not be at ease until he knew Lizinia was safe.

"We will be sure to pass along news of your good health," Peregrine said as he hugged Trix.

"And your continued existence," said Saturday. "So what do you think it is that Joy gave you?"

Trix shrugged. "I honestly have no idea."

"Well, whatever it ends up being, I just wish I could see your face when you figure it out." Saturday embraced him with vigor. Betwixt hopped beside him. Trix, careful of the majestic antlers, patted the chimera on the head.

The fete continued for some time. There was another impromptu ceremony as Falada's head was fixed to the archway of the entrance to the Faerie Hill. Trix lingered at the edge of the crowd while the Faerie Queen gave another speech, glancing over his shoulder at the Wood from time to time with a painful longing. He wanted to leave in the worst way, but he had not yet concocted a plan for escape. Even if he had, he still had no idea where to go from there.

"Once upon a time and time

A weary traveler sought a rhyme."

Trix recognized the light airy voice emanating from the trees beyond, and he broke away from the crowd to find Wednesday. Wednesday had a tendency to get lost in the Wood. Now that her mind was magic-drenched once again, Trix figured it wasn't safe to let her wander far.

But Wednesday hadn't wandered far. She was waiting for him in the berry bushes with his traveling sack, the two magic bows, and the two quivers of arrows: everything he needed to escape. Well, almost everything.

Trix pulled his distracted sister into his arms and tried not to crush her in his embrace. "I don't know if you can hear me in there, Wednesday, but I will never forget what you did. I have always thought you were wonderful and amazing, and no one will ever convince me otherwise. I hope that someday you are able to find peace again." He kissed her on the cheek. "I would offer to look for it, but I'm afraid I'm not good at that. I don't even know where to find Lizinia."

Wednesday took Trix's hands in hers and squeezed them tightly.

"My Papa's many stories told
Of leprechauns and pots of gold
And wings that lift and sand that shifts
And brave young fools who use their gifts."

For a moment Trix wished he was going home again with Saturday, to sit at Papa's knee by the fire and hear his tales of fantastical beasts and magical places and things that might have happened or not, in a time before time.

Wednesday squeezed his hands again, almost painfully this time. Had she been trying to tell him something? He tried to remember her pretty words. She had mentioned wings—might he catch a glimpse of the dragon Saturday woke?—but she'd mentioned Papa first. Papa had indeed told them many stories about leprechauns. It was a leprechaun who had originally given Papa the three fairy stones—Wednesday had turned the pink stone into a dress for Lizinia. But they hadn't been stones to begin with, they had been gold coins. Fool's gold, not that Papa had known at the time. Leprechauns loved playing tricks almost as much as they loved their gold.

Gold. Like Lizinia.

Gold.

And where could one always expect to find gold?

At the end of a rainbow.

Wednesday released Trix's hands and clapped delightedly, as if she could see the thought taking shape inside his head. With hope in his heart once more, Trix pulled Lizinia's bow off his shoulder and extracted one of her star arrows from the quiver. He quickly nocked the arrow, and then shot it high into the sky.

Wednesday yanked Trix's golden dagger from its sheath and held it above her head. Within moments, one end of a brilliant rainbow slammed down around her. The other end stretched off into the distance...incredibly far off. But at the other end of that rainbow, Trix knew, was Lizinia.

Finally, he had a direction.

Wednesday, smiling, held the golden dagger out to him. In a small, excited voice she said, "Adventure awaits."

ACKNOWLEDGEMENTS

The bulk of *Trix and the Faerie Queen* was written in November of 2015, for National Novel Writing Month. The goal of NaNoWriMo is to write 50,000 words in one month. I try to hit that goal every year, and every year I fail. This year was no different (I hit about 38,000, which is still pretty darn good!). So I must first thank everyone who participated in NaNoWriMo 2015, especially Monica Valentinelli and my dear friends the Waterworld Mermaids, who kept me sprinting to keep up my word count! (You guys are all going to join me in 2016, right?)

Beyond that, I want to thank fellow author and star-twin Lisa Mantchev, who stuck by my side through the month of January, helping me through the madness of my infamous Danny Ocean Moment and encouraging me to get down those last two chapters…that ended up becoming four.

Huge thanks to Nessa Kreyling for helping me do the business of being an author, so I could concentrate on the actual writing. (Looking forward to much more of this!)

Huge hugs and another cup of Townhouse coffee to Bianca Roman-Stumpff and Justine Birmingham, for forcing me out of my shell from time to time and reminding me that a life without art is a sad life indeed.

Thanks to Allie, Lexie, Kate, Tempest, Byron, and Matt, my partners in crime at Disney World. Getting a season pass is on my to-do list, because a princess should not have a backyard like that if she doesn't intend to make mischief once in a while!

I must also thank my crack publishing team, who banded

together to create this amazing bit of magic. My editor-star Casey Cothran, my copyeditor-star Kat Tipton, my cover-star Rachel Marks (isn't it gorgeous?), my layout-star Jason Anderson (who humors me with my drop-caps *because they are so pretty*), my narrator-star Alastair Cameron, and a special shout-out to princess-star Thea Muldrew, who did not have to mainline the entire Books of Arilland series just to give her thoughts about a book summary, but did so anyway (I wish I could write as fast as she reads!).

Forever and always, thank you to my infamous Brute Squad, who kept my spirits up through thick and thin, and won me an award to boot. What other author's street team has done that, I ask you? We are getting that picture at Dragon Con this year. Don't let me forget!

And last but not least, Mom and Dad—Marcy and George Kontis—the original Mama and Papa Woodcutter. Trix would not be the optimistic adventurer he is without you. Nor would I.

ABOUT THE AUTHOR

New York Times and USA Today bestselling author Alethea Kontis is a princess, a fairy godmother, and a geek. She's known for screwing up the alphabet, scolding vampire hunters, and ranting about fairy tales on YouTube.

Alethea's published works include: *The Wonderland Alphabet* (with Janet K. Lee), *Diary of a Mad Scientist Garden Gnome* (with Janet K. Lee), the AlphaOops series (with Bob Kolar), the Books of Arilland fairy tale series, and *The Dark-Hunter Companion* (with Sherrilyn Kenyon). Her short fiction, essays, and poetry have appeared in a myriad of anthologies and magazines.

Her YA fairy tale novel, *Enchanted*, won both the Gelett Burgess Children's Book Award and Garden State Teen Book Award. *Enchanted* was nominated for the Audie Award in 2013 and was selected for World Book Night in 2014. Both *Enchanted* and its sequel, *Hero*, were nominated for the Andre Norton Award. *Tales of Arilland*, a short story collection set in the same fairy tale world, won a second Gelett Burgess Award in 2015.

Born in Burlington, Vermont, Alethea currently lives and writes on the Space Coast of Florida. She makes the best baklava you've ever tasted and sleeps with a teddy bear named Charlie. You can find Princess Alethea on her YouTube channel, all the social media, and at her website: www.aletheakontis.com.

CPSIA information can be obtained
at www.ICGtesting.com
Printed in the USA
BVOW04*0743061216

469786BV00022B/49/P